*Harlequin
Presents..*

MARY BURCHELL

such is love

HARLEQUIN BOOKS
toronto-winnipeg

Harlequin Presents edition published October 1975
SBN 373-70611-1

Original hard cover edition published
by Mills & Boon Limited

Printed in Canada.

CHAPTER ONE

GWYNETH lifted her wedding dress from the layers of tissue paper, and held it up for a moment of admiring inspection. She had refused to let Cranston unpack the box because it was absurd to let someone else have the thrill of taking one's wedding dress from its final wrappings. And now, as the cool, shining folds slid across her bare arms, she experienced a thrill that was more strangely moving than anything she had known for a long time.

Against the mildly expressed wishes of her father, Gwyneth had chosen this pinky-parchment shade, and now she was glad. No white could have had the warmth and graciousness of this lovely shade. Canon Vilner, a conventional man, had said:

"White is the only right choice for a bride, my dear. White for virginity."

At the time, Gwyneth had wondered with a fearful curiosity what her father would have done if she had told him:

"Then, judged by that standard, I have no right to wear it."

But one never said things like that to Canon Vilner, of course. Indeed, one tried very hard not even to think of them. Because all that was so far back in the past, and if one held the page down very firmly there was no need to read again the lines which fate had written in the book of one's life.

Gwyneth shivered slightly in spite of the warm wind blowing in through the open window. It was strange and disturbing that memory could play such malicious tricks, so that even with her hand on her wedding dress—even with the image of Van so clear in her heart—she could not keep her thoughts from turning to those other days, so much better forgotten.

There was a light tap on the half-open door just then and her mother came into the room.

"Cranston said your dress had come. Dear me, Gwyneth, how really charming! You were quite right to choose that shade. And the veil? Yes, that's right too. It has a wonderfully gracious effect. Evremonde is a real artist in these matters."

"Yes," Gwyneth agreed, and that was all. Her mother often had the effect of making her reduce her conversation to monosyllables, for they had so little in common that they had remained strangers all their lives. And in spite of the fact that mother—with the exception of Aunt Eleanor—was the only person alive who knew the full story of that dark patch in Gwyneth's life.

Perhaps that was really half the trouble. Mother knew too much about her. She never said a word of it, she never even looked the faintest bit significant, for that was not Mother's way. But it was like living forever surrounded by mirrors—mirrors which reflected the past as well as the present.

One of the loveliest things about marrying Van and going right away with him was that he knew nothing about all that. One couldn't even imagine his knowing. It was a heavenly, comforting thought. When she was with him the page was turned down, and it stayed down.

Her mother, having inspected the dress and veil from every angle, turned now to the girl who was to wear them.

"I'm glad Van is so tall and distinguished. Nothing looks worse than an insignificant bridegroom beside a striking bride—and you will be that, Gwyneth, for you're a good-looking girl, thank heaven. I shouldn't have taken a tenth of the trouble I have with you if you'd been plain."

Gwyneth smiled slightly in tribute to this supposed pleasantry. But she knew it was nothing less than the cold, brutal truth. Her mother touched nothing that would not be worth touching. Self-interest ruled every action of her life with an ice-cold rod.

Gwyneth sometimes wondered how the studious, conventional man who was her father had ever come to marry her worldly mother.

"My dear, it's extraordinary that even at your age you are still perfectly capable of going off into a day-dream. The faintly irritated tone of her mother's really beautiful voice recalled Gwyneth suddenly to the fact that her thoughts had been very far away.

"I'm sorry, Mother. There's such a lot to think about just now. What were you saying?"

"I was speaking about your Aunt Eleanor."

No one could have told from Gwyneth's calm expression that the very name gave her an unspeakably disagreeable thrill.

"She has decided to come to the wedding, after all. Very tiresome of her and quite tactless, I consider, but there it is. We can't alter her decision and it's always best to accept disagreeable necessities with good grace. That's not Christianity, as your father supposes, but common sense."

"I suppose you mean she is staying here?" Gwyneth's voice was cold and a little expressionless.

"Of course. Where else would she stay? That's what I was saying. She is arriving this afternoon."

"Is she?" Gwyneth steeled herself to accept even that quietly.

"You'll have to go and fetch her from the station, my dear. Just a moment ——" Like an accomplished animal trainer, Mrs. Vilner anticipated to a nicety the detail that would make her daughter wince angrily, and she provided for it. "It can't possibly be helped. Your father has the other car. Sanders is driving him over to Chirley this afternoon. In fact, they have gone already. So there is no one else to send down with the little car except you."

"We could send a hired car for her." Gwyneth's voice quivered with feeling which was, however, well under control.

"And have her arrive thinking she had been slighted?" Mrs. Vilner shook her head and smiled faintly. "Most unwise. Don't you think so?"

Gwyneth looked at her mother. Her dark blue eyes held both pain and fear, but her mother's eyes remained cool and green and opaque. After a moment Gwyneth said:

"No doubt you're right. It's only a quarter of an hour's drive anyway. What time is her train?"

"The five-twenty. And there is no need to worry. She's as discreet as she is objectionable. You can talk of the weather and your wedding presents. She won't mention anything else."

And with this assurance, Mrs. Vilner went out of the room.

When her mother had gone, closing the door behind her, Gwyneth crossed over to the open window and sat down on the seat there. The scent of grass and clover drifted up

7

from the fields beyond the garden, and the heavy hum of a bee nearby was the only sound disturbing the silence.

So peaceful—so beautiful—so soothing.

Damn Aunt Eleanor!—and the shattering memories she brought with her. Why did she have to come all the way from Scotland to disturb the peace of one's wedding day? Why was it not possible to go to Van with a tranquil mind and memory laid to sleep? Mother didn't understand, of course. She called it a disagreeable necessity and left it at that.

Gwyneth leant her head back against the shutter and closed her eyes—and immediately time slipped away. It was more than six years ago, and a day just like this. Only she was not in her bedroom, but in the garden, and a man's arms were round her.

Not Van's arms—that was what seemed so strange now. Another man had held her in his arms and she had thought it the most wonderful thing in the world—then.

She had been only seventeen, to be sure—very little more than a child. With something like pity and the faintest touch of contempt, she could see herself now as she had been then. Romantic, passionately affectionate, seeking, almost unknowingly, for someone on whom to lavish her feelings.

There had not been a sister or brother to act as that blessed safety valve which all only children lack, and she would never have thought of either her father or her mother as a suitable confidant. Her father was too much wrapped up in his seeking after truth and learning. Her mother was too much wrapped up in herself.

In any case, at this dangerous period, they were both away on a world tour. Aunt Eleanor had come to rule in their stead over Gwyneth's destiny.

Aunt Eleanor, Canon Vilner's only sister, was, like her brother, a seeker after truth. Unlike him, she considered she had found it, and that very few other people had. This put anyone as young as Gwyneth at a serious disadvantage. She could not accept Aunt Eleanor's rather narrow, harsh ideas of truth and morality, and therefore she was wrong. To Aunt Eleanor there were no two ways about it—either you agreed with her or you were wrong.

In her way she was fond of Gwyneth. Certainly she

believed that she was, for she would have considered it definitely sinful not to be fond of her only brother's only child. But she had really not the faintest interest or understanding with regard to her niece's immature thoughts and hopes and affections.

It was a pity that Terence Muirkirk should have chosen to spend that summer sketching in the district. Even now, Gwyneth could remember the thrill of that first afternoon, when she came upon him in the glade down by the river, where she used to play as a child.

He had just glanced up from his sketching to smile at her and say:

"Hello. Does this glade belong to you?"

"Very nearly," Gwyneth had told him, because no one ever came there except herself. And she had stood there looking at him, almost afraid to go nearer.

"And do you change people into trees if they trespass here?" he wanted to know, as he reached for a tube of paint which had fallen on the grass.

"No," Gwyneth said, but she had gone nearer then, and she thought what a big, straight, handsome tree he would have made. She had never seen quite such blue eyes or quite such black hair, and she was fascinated by the ripple of muscle under the brown skin of his bare arm. Indeed, she was distinctly aware of a desire to put out her hand and touch his warm, tanned arm, just where the sleeve of his shirt was rolled above his elbow.

"Well, what *do* you do to trespassers in your magic glade?" he asked presently, still without leaving his work.

"I don't do anything to them." She sat down on the grass and looked at him with grave, transparent interest. "I see so few visitors that I'm glad when one comes."

He glanced up again then, to give her a smile that literally dazzled her.

"You don't want to chop their heads off, or anything like that?

"Oh no. May I look at what you're doing please?"

"You may." He leant a little away from his work, so that she could come, and she bent forward until her soft, golden-brown hair just touched his bare arm. She didn't know about that until he told her afterwards that that was the moment when he fell in love with her. She only knew

9

that, as she seriously examined the sketch, his voice said softly, just above her head:

"I never saw hair with so much sunshine caught in it. Are you really not a little enchanted princess?"

More than six years ago! Of course one was so thrilled by such speeches at that age. Gwyneth opened her eyes and looked round the room again.

She didn't see her wedding dress this time. She saw only the room where she had lain through hot summer nights, watching a heavy golden moon move slowly across the sky. By day she wandered in the woods and along the river bank, accompanied—so Aunt Eleanor believed—only by her dog and a copy of Bacon's essays, which she was supposed to read as a holiday task.

But Gwyneth's dog ran just where he pleased, and Bacon's essays remained almost unopened. For Terry walked at her side, or lay sometimes with his head in her lap, while he taught her very much more about love than was to be found in Bacon's essay on marriage.

They were happy, feverish, bewildering days and unhappy, feverish, bewildering nights, because every hour spent away from Terry was an hour wasted.

When he told her she would have to steal away with him secretly if they were ever to marry and be together, she believed him, and she thought she had found perfect joy at last.

He was right, of course—her parents would never dream of letting her marry a penniless artist before she was out of her teens. But when the deed was accomplished, and there was nothing to gain by withholding their approval—then her parents would become resigned to facts and discover for themselves how enchanting Terry was.

In this very room she had packed her things for the tragi-romantic adventure. On that table by her bed she had left the silly, melodramatic little note for Aunt Eleanor. And then she had stolen down the stairs, out into the warm, moonlit night, to where Terry was waiting for her in the deep patch of shadow at the end of the drive.

Two weeks—three weeks—was that really all the time it had taken to disillusion her completely? No, perhaps a few frightened hopes had lingered even after that, or else the final, shattering discovery could scarcely have hurt so much.

The first suspicion came with that horrid scene when he was so angry at discovering she had come without her jewellery. It had seemed to her such a small point. She could do without jewellery—even without the few very good pieces left to her by her grandmother, and of which she was genuinely fond.

But Terry had been furious—called her a stupid, unworldly little thing. And even though she pointed out that later on, when they were reconciled with her parents, she could easily collect her jewellery again, he remained unmollified. It was so difficult to imagine why. The whole thing seemed so unnecessary. And she was not entirely comforted by the passionate, disturbing scene of reconciliation which came later.

She loved him, of course. She wanted to be his. But there were some things about Terry's love-making which shocked and even horrified her. Perhaps it was a little because she scarcely felt married to him. That hurried business at the register office, with a lie about her age and a few half-truths about other particulars, was sadly unlike a wedding as she knew the meaning of the word.

Still, she must try to look at these things in a more sophisticated way, as Terry said. It was absurd to argue everything from the childish premises which he seemed to find now more irritating than endearing.

So Gwyneth struggled on through the wretched weeks, trying not to see that it was disillusionment, not knowledge, which was growing upon her, and that the romantic dream had passed into a sordid awakening.

Gwyneth got up suddenly and, crossing the room, began to move some of the things on her dressing-table. There was nothing there which needed re-arranging really, but even now she could not bear to sit still while her mind went over that final scene.

Perhaps she had understood, even before that, that the man she had married was worthless and selfish and cruel. She had not understood that he was nothing but a common swindler, and a bigamist.

No wonder he had raged when she left home without her jewellery. That was to be the profitable part of the bargain. The rest—the enjoyment of a young, untried girl, still with the first bloom on her—had been a secondary consideration. He had tired of her even before his real wife turned up and made that hideous scene.

They had said things Gwyneth had never forgotten—used words she hoped never to hear again. And then they had gone out and left her—sitting stunned and wordless amid the ruins of her life.

Perhaps the most sordid and ridiculous detail of all was that she had to pay the bill for their hotel. The management were very polite but very firm about that. The gentleman had said she would settle the bill before leaving. They understood he had had to leave urgently on business and that she was joining him later.

She paid. But she didn't join the gentleman later. She had never set eyes on Terry again. Perhaps he went to South America, after all. He had spoken of it with the dreadful woman who said she was his wife. But, in any case, he dropped as completely from her life as if he had been shot, as he deserved.

Now, looking back on him dispassionately, she could think that. He should have been shot. But then, of course, she had grown harder with the years, and she thought things now that would have made her shiver when she was younger.

That seemed an odd thing to say of oneself at twenty-three or four—except that one could not measure age by years alone. For instance, she had felt forty or fifty when she dragged her way back to Aunt Eleanor at the end of those tragic few weeks.

It was hard to recollect now just how she had stammered out the story. It took a very long while, because Aunt Eleanor refused to understand implications. One had to give the whole thing in black and white.

At the end, she had just remarked bitterly, like some absurd character in a goody-goody story:

"Then all these weeks you have been living in sin?"

"I thought I was married," Gwyneth had said faintly, but Aunt Eleanor merely repeated:

"You have been living in sin." And, in the end, Gwyneth had to admit that she *had*.

Aunt Eleanor sent her to bed after that—whether on health grounds or as a punishment, Gwyneth had never been able to decide. Aunt Eleanor would see nothing incongruous in banishing an erring niece to bed, even if that niece had grown up sufficiently to live with a man as his wife for several weeks.

Gwyneth had lain there all that dreary evening, in the room where she had dreamed such romantic, heart-warming dreams. Yes—still this very same room where her wedding dress now hung, ready for her to wear when she married Van on Thursday.

Very late in the evening Aunt Eleanor had come and asked if she were awake, and Gwyneth, who felt she would never sleep again, admitted in a whisper that she was.

"We have got to decide what we are going to do about this terrible business." Sitting there in the half-light, Aunt Eleanor had looked absurdly unlike a conspirator—but she proved herself a masterly tactician.

"I have written absolutely nothing to your parents about your wicked running away," Aunt Eleanor announced. "So far as they are concerned, you have never left home."

"They—know—nothing?" she gasped, hardly daring to put the discovery into words. "Oh, Aunt Eleanor, how good of you! How wonderfully good of you!"

"It was not for your sake that I kept silent," Aunt Eleanor told her sharply. "It was for my poor brother, whose heart would certainly be broken if he knew what you have been doing." She said a great deal more about her brother's broken heart, though nothing at all about Gwyneth's. But perhaps that was understandable.

"The servants think you were away on an unexpected visit. At least, I have told them that," Aunt Eleanor added, with a grimness that would have forbidden speculation. "The few friends who inquired were told the same thing. I have sent what excuses I could to your parents for your not having written, and I hope you have not been such a fool as to write to them."

"No," Gwyneth whispered. "I waited to see what attitude they wanted to take."

"Thank God," Aunt Eleanor said, and she meant it quite literally. She thanked Him sincerely for having looked after her affairs so well, and for having inspired her niece with a grain of sense in all this welter of sinful absurdity.

"Then—nobody really knows?" Gwyneth lay back again, feeling very weak and queer.

"Nobody—except you and me."

"Aunt Eleanor, can it really—remain like that?"

"So long as you have the good sense to hold your tongue," was the sharp retort. "*I* shall certainly not go tattling about anything so disgraceful. How the daughter of your father and mother could ever have come to such a pass——" She broke off, because words did indeed fail to clothe her surprise and fury. Gwyneth closed her eyes, in order to shut out her aunt's hard, angry expression.

"Your parents will be home in a fortnight's time," Aunt Eleanor's voice informed her warningly. "I had a letter from them yesterday. By that time, I hope you will have contrived to look your usual self again."

So she had two weeks in which to grow back to the unknowing seventeen-year-old who had never even been kissed—let alone lain in a man's arms, learning passion and desire, and disillusionment.

And she managed it. Incredible though it seemed, she had played the part so well that nothing was suspected in the two months which followed her parents' return home. There were few things later than A.D. 150 which commanded her father's complete attention, in any case, and her mother was always primarily concerned with her own immediate affairs.

It had been a week after Aunt Eleanor's departure that the growing suspicion in Gwyneth's mind took on a horrible certainty. Aunt Eleanor might have planned magnificently. Gwyneth herself might have acted splendidly. But concealment was, after all, an impossibility. Those weeks with Terry were not to slip into the gulf of time, leaving no trace behind. Gwyneth was going to have his child.

Even now, she could remember the fearful, clammy chill which settled on her as she admitted the truth to herself. It had been almost like looking death in the face. She had sat here on the side of her bed, slowly rubbing the palms of her hands together in a sort of subconscious effort to bring some warmth to her chilled being.

She had thought disjointedly of suicide, of running away —only that was too much like the flight with Terry—of day-to-day concealment and deception. And then she had known suddenly that she could not possibly face any of those. There was one course, and one course only. With a

14

determination which even now surprised her when she thought of it, she had gone to her mother and told her the whole story.

This time there was no stammering, no half-whispered confession, as there had been with Aunt Eleanor. Just a cold, bald recital of the facts. Gwyneth had not only grown up in those last few weeks. She had grown hard—with a sort of desperate, weary hardness which meant that somehow the spring was broken.

Mother's reception of the story had been characteristic. Like Aunt Eleanor, she, too, said at once: "Your father must not know." But she didn't add anything about breaking his heart, because Mother never concerned herself with anything like that. She said:

"We couldn't possibly keep it quiet if he knew."

That, to her, was the important point. And by a different path, she arrived at conclusions identical with Aunt Eleanor's.

The ethics of the case commanded only a fraction of her attention, but the offence against common sense made her coldly furious.

"What sort of judgment have you got, you little fool," she had asked in that soft, beautiful voice of hers, "to go running about the countryside with a penniless bounder who was afraid even to face your parents? Didn't even that give you some hint to keep away from register offices and cheap hotels with him?"

Gwyneth had had no answer ready for that, and her mother had not expected any. *She* was prepared to find the answers to the problems confronting them. And she did find them all.

Canon Vilner was told—with a wealth of convincing detail—that his daughter was run down and must have a long rest in the quiet Highland retreat which was Aunt Eleanor's home. For a man who believed he actively sought after truth, he accepted the lie with rather pathetic readiness, Gwyneth thought. And, with very little delay, she had been packed off North, to spend the waiting months with Aunt Eleanor.

Aunt Eleanor had rented a cottage even more remote from civilization than her own home, and, as her sole attendant, she engaged an elderly woman who had once been a district nurse, but who had long ago been forced by deafness to give up her occupation.

And with only this strange, silent woman and Aunt Eleanor for company, Gwyneth had spent the months waiting for her baby's arrival. All the time——

"Miss Vilner." There was a knock at the door, and with an almost physical start, Gwyneth came back from her memories of sombre Highland glens to the warm sunshine of her own bedroom.

"Yes, Cranston?"

"Madam said for you not to forget that you are taking the car to meet the five-twenty. It's five to five now."

"All right. Thank you, Cranston."

The five-twenty—and Aunt Eleanor. She would have to hurry. She couldn't indulge in memories any longer. And who wanted to, anyway? What was the good—what was the good? It was all past and done with. Why could she never persuade herself to believe that? Mother believed it —even Aunt Eleanor believed it. They had *made* it so, themselves. The past was dead.

Gwyneth reached for her powder blue coat and tied a blue scarf over her hair. She scarcely glanced at herself in the mirror—at the slim, sophisticated, faintly enigmatic creature who had made Evander Onslie suddenly decide that women *had* a place in his life after all—even if he were a powerful, cool-thinking steel magnate.

So different, so indescribably different, from the girl who had captured Terry Muirkirk's wandering fancy more than six years ago. Still the same soft brown hair with 'sunshine caught in it', still the wide-set blue eyes that darkened or lightened with every change of mood, still the faintly golden bloom on her skin and the touch of colour where her cheeks hollowed slightly under the wide cheek-bones. But the mouth was different. That was what changed her so much. No longer was it soft and pliant, ready to curve upwards in the half-placatory smile of her girlhood. It was cool and firm and very faintly hard, and often when Gwyneth smiled now, an observer might have wondered a little uneasily just what knowledge lay behind that smile.

She went out of the room and down the wide, sunny staircase. Outside the open front door stood her own little dark blue sports car, and getting into the car, she glanced up at the windows of the house to see if her mother were watching. There was no sign of her, but that did not banish the queer feeling Gwyneth always had that her mother did watch her, and the faint, involuntary shrug which she gave was really her assurance to herself that she didn't care anyway.

The dark blue car shot down the drive, slowed at the gate as it turned into the country road, and then stopped altogether. At the same moment a tall figure in grey flannels crossed from the footpath and came to a standstill beside her.

"Hello, Van."

"Hello, my dear. Where are you off to now?"

"Only to the station to meet Aunt Eleanor."

"And Aunt Eleanor is the grim lady from the Highlands, isn't she? I thought she was not coming to our wedding."

"She wasn't, but now she is. First thoughts were best, but it can't be helped." Gwyneth smiled up at her fiancé as he towered above her.

At seventeen, she would have been awed and possibly repelled by Evander Onslie. At twenty-three, she found him so disturbingly dear that sometimes she was half afraid, because he meant so much to her.

She loved the slight smile that often softened his very firm mouth when he looked at her. She loved his tall figure and his dark hair, slightly greying at the temples. She knew that other people were a good deal afraid of those direct, uncompromising dark eyes, and the stern, often abrupt manner. But, oddly enough, she was not. There was something clear-cut and astringent about everything he did and said, and that in itself gave her a sense of security.

"I'm sorry about the aunt," he said with that slight smile. "That is, if she really vexes you. But it would take more than an aunt to spoil Thursday, I think."

Gwyneth laughed, and Aunt Eleanor immediately became less menacing.

"She doesn't matter, really. Were you going up to the house, Van?"

"Yes. I wanted to see your father about one or two things."

"He's not in, I'm afraid."

"Not? Then I'll come in later and see him just before dinner."

"Yes, do. I must go now or I shall be keeping Aunt Eleanor waiting, and that's the eighth deadly sin."

Gwyneth pressed the self-starter and tossed him a farewell smile.

"See you in an hour or two." And the car was off down the road once more.

She was terribly glad she had seen him. Somehow it took the sting out of all the dreadful memories which Aunt Eleanor's coming had evoked. He represented her new world, her absolutely fresh beginning. The years which had passed were nothing but a bridge between. At this end stood Van—quiet, strong, sane. At the far end, a confused group composed of Aunt Eleanor, the deaf woman who said almost nothing, later her mother and an elderly doctor from a village five miles from the cottage.

With a little groan of impatience, Gwyneth realized she had crossed the bridge again. Van hadn't banished the memories, after all. She had picked up her train of thought exactly where she had dropped it when Cranston had summoned her just now.

Well then, *let* her thoughts run on! If she set her teeth and went over every inch of the way, perhaps that would lay the ghosts at last. Didn't psychologists have some theory like that? You faced the fears buried deep in your subconscious mind—and then they didn't exist any longer.

Fears! Yes, fear was the overwhelming impression from that night she was remembering now. Fear of the future, fear of the raging storm outside which delayed the doctor, fear of the pain which came in sickening, paralysing waves —fear of death which, she knew with certainty, stood very near.

Frowning slightly, Gwyneth stared ahead down the dusty road, not seeing the fields or the hedges or the sunlight, but only the little cottage bedroom where her child had been born. It seemed a strange, far-off delirious kind of dream now. And at the time, it had scarcely been any more real. She could hardly believe that the central figure had been herself. The whole thing had been just the culmination of the impossible unrealities which had happened to her over a period of a year. The climax of a ghastly nightmare from which it was quite impossible to wake up —until suddenly the baby—her baby—was in the world and a real being at last.

Until the moment when she heard it crying she had never thought of it as a person at all. She had accepted her mother's and Aunt Eleanor's view that, along with all the other circumstances of this unhappy business, the child must be firmly ruled out of any future she might try to build.

A great many things had been said about the imperative need for secrecy, the impossibility of Canon Vilner's daughter appearing before the world as an unmarried mother, the excellent and immediate arrangements that could and would be made.

Gwyneth had silently acquiesced in all this when they talked things over before the baby came. They were right, of course, Mother and Aunt Eleanor. For her father's sake, for her own future's sake, even for the child's sake, it was better that this terrible episode should be finally and irrevocably closed. The arguments had all seemed so good at the time. In an orphanage the child would grow up just like all the other children round it, unaware of any difference. In any other circumstances it could only be an unhappy little outcast.

She had quite seen the common sense of it all—in theory. The only difficulty was that everything altered completely when she first heard that rather weak little wail, and saw the small fluffy head of the baby she had borne.

To this day, Gwyneth supposed, Mother and Aunt Eleanor considered that some madness of delirium had descended on her immediately after the baby's birth. There had been the most terrible scene—Gwyneth insisting with the violence of despair that she must keep her child after all, that she didn't believe in the force of their arguments any more, and Mother and Aunt Eleanor holding to their first decision.

It had ended, as it was almost bound to end, with terrifying collapse on Gwyneth's part, and a few days of illness so severe that she knew nothing at all of what was going on round her.

The car turned into the small station yard. She was five minutes too early after all and, pulling up, she leaned her

19

arms on the wheel and sat gazing along the winding railway track where Aunt Eleanor's train would come.

The outlines of the scene seemed to quiver a little in the afternoon heat, and Gwyneth closed her eyes.

She remembered that afternoon when she had slowly come back to life again. She had lain there in bed, watching the grey sky through the window, and planning how she would persuade her mother and Aunt Eleanor instead of forcing them, as she had tried to do in her hysterical despair. She would explain that she was willing to go away somewhere and live very quietly for the rest of her life, if only she might keep the baby. No scandal should invade her father's world. She would even go abroad if necessary—

She had had her case almost complete by the time her mother had come in to see her. But it had all been quite unnecessary, after all. With a brusqueness which perhaps was kinder than evasion, her mother had explained that the problem had solved itself. During the days when Gwyneth had been so ill, her weakly little baby had died.

And there the terrible episode with Terry had finally ended. A great blankness and emptiness had seemed to succeed that tragic year, and then a very different Gwyneth had emerged from the fire of experience—the sophisticated, cool, slightly hard Gwyneth whom Evander Onslie had met, much later, and asked to marry him.

The local train puffed slowly into the station, as though rather pleased with itself that once more it had negotiated that slope successfully. Aunt Eleanor and two other passengers descended. One was a large, hot, gaitered farmer, and the other a scrawny little woman weighed down by innumerable parcels.

But, in any case, neither of them counted for anything beside Aunt Eleanor. She was not very fashionably dressed and there was nothing about her to suggest vulgar prosperity, but she was such a perfect, perfect lady that it was only with the greatest diffidence that the stationmaster (now ticket-collector) ventured to ask her for her ticket.

By that time she had already pecked conventionally at her niece's cheek and said:

"Well, Gwyneth, how d'you do? You certainly look better than last time I saw you"—quite as though 'last

20

time' had not been five years ago and the circumstances such as one might have preferred to forget.

Gwyneth assured her aunt coolly that her health was now excellent and inquired dutifully after her own.

"Nothing to complain of," retorted Aunt Eleanor, a little as though she was graciously absolving the Almighty from any blame. "Some rheumatism sometimes, but at sixty-five one must expect that." And she climbed into the car with an agility out of keeping with her statement about her age.

The stationmaster (now in his capacity as porter) put her luggage in the back of the car, Gwyneth gave him a slight smile and a nod of thanks, and then drove the car away from the station at the decorous twenty-five miles an hour which Aunt Eleanor considered a sufficiently dashing speed.

"Thank you very much for the silver candlesticks, Aunt Eleanor," Gwyneth began, mindful perhaps of her mother's remark that wedding presents made a safe topic of conversation. "They are really beautiful."

"Genuine Georgian. Exquisite things," said Aunt Eleanor, who saw no reason whatever to disparage her own generosity.

"Yes, I could see they were. Van admired them very much, too. He is very fond of old silver."

There was silence for a moment, then Aunt Eleanor said:

"So you're going to marry Evander Onslie. He is rather old for you, but an excellent match."

"Van is only thirty-five," Gwyneth informed her curtly.

"Quite. Eleven and a half years older than you," Aunt Eleanor insisted. "A little old for you, as I remarked." And conversation languished once more.

Presently Gwyneth tried again.

"We have had some very lovely presents. You'll have to come and see them in the library after dinner."

"I should like to. Are there many guests coming to the wedding?"

"About a hundred."

Aunt Eleanor gave a sigh of satisfaction.

"And the Bishop is marrying you, of course?"

"Oh yes."

"And to think that once——" Aunt Eleanor broke off, and then added pointedly: "You have great reason to be thankful to your mother and me, Gwyneth."

"I hope I am not ungrateful," Gwyneth said so dryly that her aunt observed a little stiffly:

"I find something of a change in you."

"One must change a good deal between eighteen and twenty-three, I suppose." Gwyneth made that sound light and careless, and a puzzled look flickered over Aunt Eleanor's face.

"What sort of man is Evander Onslie?" was her next inquiry.

"To look at, do you mean?"

"Good gracious, no!" Personal appearance was of less than no importance to Aunt Eleanor. "Is he grave or gay —frivolous or responsible, a decent, God-fearing man or a scoundrel like ——?"

"He is not a scoundrel," Gwyneth interrupted coldly. "And he is not in the least frivolous. I don't know whether he's afraid of God, but I shouldn't think so. I can't imagine Van at all afraid of anything."

"Then he ought to be!" retorted Aunt Eleanor. "A decent fear of God is what keeps most people straight."

"I don't think religious terrorism would appeal to Van as either decent or sensible," Gwyneth said coolly, "but I imagine his general principles would satisfy you, Aunt Eleanor. He has a certain sense of humour but is stern about what you would call The Things That Matter."

A faint, harsh flush crept into Aunt Eleanor's cheeks.

"I think, as your only aunt, Gwyneth, I am entitled to tell you that you have not at all improved with the years," she said sharply. "Hard flippancy and callous disregard of serious matters are revolting in a girl of your age. Very fashionable, perhaps—but revolting."

"I'm sorry, Aunt Eleanor." Gwyneth *was* conscious of regret that she had shocked her aunt quite so far, but it was difficult to remember the degree of docility and meekness which she had been able to produce in the old days. "Perhaps I don't mean quite all I say," she offered placatorily.

"Then why say it?" snapped Aunt Eleanor unanswerably.

"That in itself indicates an irresponsible, unbalanced attitude of mind."

Gwyneth didn't offer to explain further. For one thing, she felt faintly ashamed of herself, and for another, they were nearing the house now and she didn't want to prolong the argument.

Canon Vilner had already returned home when they arrived, and as the car drove up, he opened the door himself and came down the steps to greet his sister.

Although nearly sixty, he was still tall and straight and an exceedingly handsome man—his completely white hair only adding to that distinguished bearing which still made elderly, susceptible ladies refer to 'his fine head'.

"My dear Eleanor"—he kissed his sister rather impressively on both cheeks—"I am very glad indeed to see you. I hope you will forgive me for urging you to come so far, but I should not have liked my little girl to have this important day of her life without her aunt being present to see her happiness."

His little girl stood by, smiling slightly. So it was her father who had urged Aunt Eleanor to change her first politic decision not to come. Well, of course, that was understandable, since he was completely in the dark about the real state of affairs.

"Well, my dear, this is a very pleasant surprise for you. We hardly dared to hope your Aunt Eleanor would come all the way from the north of Scotland, did we?"

"No. It's very kind of her indeed," Gwyneth agreed, with what she hoped was an adequate appearance of having shared her father's ardent hopes that Aunt Eleanor *would* come.

Then they went into the house, to be greeted by Mrs. Vilner, and the little comedy was repeated, only much more convincingly this time because Mother was rather better at these things than Gwyneth.

Fortunately, Gwyneth was considered to have 'a great many things still to do,' and so she was able to make her escape soon after this, leaving Canon Vilner to enjoy the society of his sister quite sincerely, and his wife to conceal her dislike under a pleasantly smiling mask.

In her bedroom once more, Gwyneth wrote one or two last-minute letters and then began to dress leisurely for dinner. She put on the cream wool with the great corn-flower-blue flowers splashed over it. It was not a new dress, but Van liked it. He said the blue was the colour of her eyes, and the cream the colour of her throat. Van didn't often make such remarks, and she treasured this one all the more for that.

In her ears she put small pearl drop earrings. She had not worn earrings in the days when Aunt Eleanor had known her before, and she hoped, with half-humorous regret, that they would not evoke any disapproval. In any case, they were in keeping with her older, more sophisticated style now, and gave her a touch of authority and dignity which one might reasonably expect to find in Evander Onslie's wife.

With little of the misgiving which would have assailed her once, Gwyneth hoped that she was going to fit well into that rather responsible position. To be the wife of one of the biggest industrialists in the country was a responsibility, she supposed. But if Van, at thirty-five, was not overwhelmed by his position as head of the great Onslie Steel Works, she, at twenty-three, must not fear her position as his wife.

Van's wife! The very phrase gave her an exquisite sense of happiness, and slowly the last shadows of the past seemed to give way before the sunshine of the future. Van's wife —she was marrying him in two days' time—and there hung her wedding dress as tangible proof of the fact.

It was hard to believe that six months ago she had not even met him. When she had seen him at the Courtenays' New Year party that first week-end, he had seemed familiar to her, probably from some half-remembered newspaper photograph. But until he was introduced, she had not been able to identify him. Then, when she had heard his name, she had thought.:

"Evander Onslie! One of those big businessmen. Not my sort at all. Much too grim and serious."

But if Van were serious and—yes, even quite often grim, he certainly had his own way of unbending at times.

He unbent for her. There was no question about it. No one else in the room seemed to interest him after he had bowed over her hand.

Sceptical and a little cynical now where masculine admiration was concerned, Gwyneth had not been encouraging. She had resolutely kept things on a light and careless basis.

He was puzzled, she saw, and not a little angry, but quite undismayed. He invited himself down to the Courtenays' place the next week-end—and again, the next. Then he proposed to her—and she refused him.

She had supposed he would accept that, but she was much mistaken. He took a week-end cottage of his own in the neighbourhood, and proposed again.

"I've told you 'no'," Gwyneth pointed out with her cool smile. "Perhaps you've never met the word before?"

"At any rate, I don't know its meaning in connection with you." He brushed her protest aside without even a smile. "Any man who takes 'no' from the woman he loves doesn't deserve to win her. In any case, I never take 'no' when I'm determined."

"Really? Well, I'm not a steel contract, you know." Gwyneth had told him. "I don't know that business methods are going to assist here."

He had taken her in his arms then, whether she liked it or not, and said:

"No, you're not a steel contract. You're a golden dream. But I don't take 'no' all the same. I've moved too quickly —I see that now. But I'll wait. There is such a thing as siege as well as attack."

That hadn't been the end, of course, but it had been the beginning of the end, and a month later she had been wearing Van's diamond on her engagement finger.

Only then had she wondered how much of the past she ought to tell him. And, after a night of tormenting uncertainty and self-questioning, she had decided definitely— nothing, nothing, nothing.

Perhaps it was difficult to say now how much or how little she had been to blame in that horrible episode of her youth. But one thing was quite certain—*nothing* could make it sound anything but sordid and dreadful, once one put it into words. One could not expect Van, with his uncompromising outlook, to regard it as anything else.

Her past was *her* past. She had no need to lie—only to keep silent. And the two people in the world who knew her story would keep silent, too. Of that she was certain. Nowadays she was strong enough to keep her own counsel, strong enough even to forget—almost. And perhaps, in the new and happy life with Van, she would learn to forget altogether.

She was glad he was coming to dinner tonight. She realized, with some amusement for her own ingenuousness, that she was so proud of him that she wanted to show him off even to Aunt Eleanor.

Gwyneth glanced at the silver clock on her table.

Twenty past seven. He would be here any moment now. She had better go down.

And then she remembered—he was going to have a talk with her father. Then, perhaps, she had better do her duty as a niece and go and make herself pleasant to Aunt Eleanor. She could show her the presents in the library and let her see for herself how handsome her own offering looked.

But when Gwyneth knocked on the door of her aunt's room, she found she had already gone downstairs, presumably to the library.

The door of the house stood open and there was a beautiful glimpse of the garden, gracious and sleepy in the warm evening light. From her father's study came the sound of voices. That would be Van and he talking.

Gwyneth felt very happy and curiously tranquil. Afterwards, she used to think of it as the quiet before the storm, but at that moment she only thought that perhaps the searching of past memories had really laid some ghosts and given her peace of mind.

More slowly she went through to the back of the house where the library was. Here, too, there was a murmur of voices. Evidently Mother was before her and *she* was dutifully showing the presents to Aunt Eleanor.

Gwyneth was tempted to leave her mother to it, and snatch a quiet ten minutes alone in the garden. But that would be rather a shame. She paused just outside the slightly open door, and as she did so, her aunt's voice drifted to her.

"Sandra," (that was Mother's absurdly melodramatic name, but it suited her), "either you are utterly insensitive or you have no appreciation of danger."

26

"Oh," thought Gwyneth amusedly, "so Mother is going through it now. Had I better go in or——?"

"I am not aware of any danger," Mother's beautiful voice stated coolly and positively.

"But don't you understand that it's the very same orphanage? *The very same.* Evander Onslie is one of the head trustees of Greystones."

For some reason she couldn't define, Gwyneth suddenly found her heart beating high up in her throat. She was frightened at the noise it seemed to be making—frightened, in case she should not hear mother's next words. But they came quite clearly to her.

"Very well. Van is a trustee of Greystones. What about it? For what earthly reason should Gwyneth suppose that Greystones has any significance for her?"

With a hand that shook slightly, Gwyneth pushed open the door and went into the library. Aunt Eleanor was standing by one of the long tables where the presents had been laid out, her expression angry and agitated. Mrs. Vilner was leaning back in an armchair regarding her with an air of tolerant amusement.

At the sound of Gwyneth's entrance, they both turned their eyes on her, and while her mother's face became quite blank, Aunt Eleanor's paled slightly.

Gwyneth shut the door and leant against it—partly because she felt she needed some support.

"Aunt Eleanor," she said very quickly, "will you tell me why Greystones Orphanage should have any significance for me?"

CHAPTER TWO

Aunt Eleanor opened her mouth, gasped slightly, and closed it again.

"My dear," Gwyneth's mother said smoothly, "what are you talking about? The place has no significance for you at all, apart from the fact that Eleanor was just telling me she understands Van is a trustee of it."

"And that fact agitated Aunt Eleanor very much. Why? And you were reassuring her with the statement that I was ignorant of any significance it had for me. Why?"

"You are imagining things," Mrs. Vilner said coldly.

27

"And you are lying," Gwyneth retorted brutally. "Aunt Eleanor, will you speak to me? I am asking you. You're more afraid of lying than Mother is. You must tell me the truth."

"Gwyneth—really, my dear—it's quite absurd—and you're being extremely rude to your mother."

"Rude!" Gwyneth laughed rather harshly. "*Rude!* What does that matter at a moment like this?" She came slowly forward into the room, her eyes never leaving her aunt's agitated face. "Never mind about the orphanage, then. I want you to answer another question instead. It's simpler and it's much more vital. Did my baby really—die, or was that just another of Mother's lies?"

"Really, Gwyneth, I never heard such—Sandra——" Aunt Eleanor's eyes sought those of her sister-in-law almost imploringly.

"No, don't ask Mother's assistance. Just answer my question. Yes or no?" Gwyneth knew that her aunt could keep a secret so long as she was not questioned, but she genuinely quailed before a flat lie.

Behind her, she could almost feel her mother's cold anger, but she refused to be intimidated. She simply stared at her aunt and repeated quite gently:

"Did my baby die—or is he still alive?—at Greystones, perhaps?"

"Gwyneth—it's most terribly unfortunate—so much better that you should never know—all over years ago really. You must just think of him as dead, child——" Aunt Eleanor's voice stammered into silence.

Gwyneth took no more notice of her. She swung round to face her mother, who still leant back in her chair, regarding the scene with a slight smile which concealed her fury.

"You hateful, wicked woman," Gwyneth said slowly. "So you settled all that, and then covered your tracks by lying to me when I was too ill to do anything but believe you."

Her mother remained unmoved, though Aunt Eleanor's gasp showed the measure of her horrors at such words being addressed to a parent.

"Don't be absurd, my dear." Mrs. Vilner kept her voice quite low, just as Gwyneth herself did. "Why behave like

28

someone in *East Lynn?* And still more, why blame me? I did what was much the best thing for us all, at a time when you were certainly not in a fit state to make your own decisions."

"You lied to me." Again Gwyneth's voice sounded almost harsh.

"And why not? Would you have been any happier during the last five years if you had known the truth?"

"I had a right to know the truth and judge for myself."

"You *had* judged, Gwyneth. You had consented to what I did, in the months before the child was born. Do you suppose I was going to have all our careful arrangements shattered for the sake of an hysterical outburst of sentiment? You were too ill to reason clearly. You simply didn't know at that time what was best, or what was absolutely impossible."

"The—the baby's coming changed that."

"Oh no. I'm no believer in these last-minute miracles of mother-love," Mrs. Vilner retorted with a slight curl of her lip. "The baby's coming changed nothing. Exposure would still have ruined your future, put your father in an unbearable position, meant endless unpleasantness for me, and done very little—if anything—for the child. None of that was changed at all. The only thing which had changed was *your* attitude. Sentiment got the better of common sense. So, for your own sake, if nothing else, I *had* to make this decision for you. And I maintain you have been happier for it. You have been able to build your life again because of it."

"How plausible you make it all sound," Gwyneth exclaimed bitterly. "But it doesn't really alter anything."

She looked at her mother with an expression of baffled dislike that was naked in its frankness. Most women would have quailed before such a glance from a daughter, but Mrs. Vilner never flinched.

"Well, my dear, the justification of my choice is that the day after tomorrow, with your—past, shall we say?— satisfactorily buried, you are going to marry Van Onslie. How do you suppose the presence of an illegitimate child would have affected *that?*

Gwyneth started.

She had forgotten Van for the moment. Indeed, she had

forgotten everything but this overwhelming disclosure. As though shutting out something she had not the courage to face, she pressed her hands over her eyes.

There was silence in the room, while Mrs. Vilner and Aunt Eleanor exchanged a glance. Then Aunt Eleanor spoke.

"You must see it has all been for the best, Gwyneth."

A convulsive little movement from her niece was the only protest against this, but at least there were not the fierce reproaches there had been at first.

Gwyneth's thoughts were working in quick, panic-stricken flashes. What was she going to do? Drag everything into the open? Announce, two days before her wedding, that she had an illegitimate child? Wreck Van's happiness—her father's position—her own happiness? Set about finding her child? While the wedding guests were put off and sordid explanations made to the Bishop—presumably by her unfortunate father—she was to go to this orphanage and make inquiries about a child who had always been brought up as an orphan anyway? It was incredible.

These were arguments that Mother would have used, of course—cold, clear-cut, ruthless. But they had the terrible ring of common sense.

Then the moment of dramatic silence was broken by the sound of the dinner gong.

"What are you going to do, Gwyneth?" Mrs. Vilner asked very quietly.

Gwyneth passed the tip of her tongue over her dry lips.

"I don't know," she said rather heavily. "I simply don't know."

"Well, please do nothing rash or hurried." The sharpness of her mother's voice showed suddenly that her nerves, too, were over-strained. "Remember that a word can ruin everything—and nothing can build the future a second time."

"I'll remember," Gwyneth said. And on that they went in to dinner.

It was a terrible meal.

Van was almost unaware of anything wrong—the Canon completely so, but neither Gwyneth nor Aunt Eleanor played her role particularly well. Mother was much better

30

at it, and engaged Van most of the time in light conversation which did not, however, entirely distract his attention from his silent fiancée.

Once or twice Gwyneth knew that Van's dark eyes rested on her with a rather thoughtful expression, but she was powerless to look at him in return and give him the reassuring smile he expected.

She was not surprised that, immediately after dinner, when they moved into the big drawing-room overlooking the garden, he came over to her and said abruptly:

"Let's go into the garden for a while, Gwyneth. It's much too lovely to spend the whole evening indoors."

She went—aware that both her aunt and her mother hid their deep anxiety with difficulty. Mother no doubt was thinking: "This will be too much for the little fool. She'll make some sort of confession now." While Aunt Eleanor was probably already almost resigned to the exposure of the whole miserable business, and was wondering—as she wondered about everything—how it would affect her brother.

As they stepped out of the french window and turned along the path which bordered the shrubbery, Van drew her arm lightly through his.

"What is wrong, my dear?" His tone was quiet but quite determined.

"Nothing, Van."

He evidently didn't accept that, because he simply waited calmly for her to add something else.

After a moment she tried again.

"Do you mean—why am I cross and silent?"

He smiled slightly.

"No. Why are you unhappy and silent?"

"Aunt Eleanor ruffled me rather," Gwyneth said with an effort.

"Did she?" For a moment those dark eyes were on her again in silently disconcerting surprise. "It isn't like you to let anyone annoy you so much. Was it something definite or——?"

"No. I don't like her much, you know—nor what she says, and the—the way she reminds me of things I'd rather forget."

31

Van gave a short laugh which most women would have found frightening rather than reassuring, but he drew her into the circle of his arm, and, in spite of everything, she felt better when she was close against him like that. "What does she remind you of? Stormy days at school?—or early struggles for independence?" He was evidently not taking the matter very seriously.

"No. She makes me feel—feel unworthy of you."

"How very ridiculous of her," Van said coolly. "And how very ridiculous of you to take any notice. Is that all the trouble?"

"Perhaps—perhaps there's something in what she says."

"I think not."

There was a silence, still quite calm on his part. Then Gwyneth sighed.

"You're not at all a suspicious man, are you, Van?" She spoke a little as though she couldn't help it.

"Not at all," he agreed. "At least, not where the people I love are concerned. I don't think love is worth much without trust. But why do you ask? Do you want me to prove the depth of my devotion by being jealous and suspicious?"

"No, of course not!"

She smiled faintly and pressed against him. It was somehow an almost childlike gesture and oddly pathetic. Van looked down at her and his mouth softened.

"Then what?"

"I was wondering whether——" She broke off, and then started again. "You don't think that when two people marry there ought to be a sort of owning up to anything that went before?—So that you start clear, I mean."

"No, my dear, I don't!" Van's smile was dry and he spoke with great firmness. "I can imagine nothing more profitless and unpleasant than raking over old flirtations which should have been decently buried long ago. I don't doubt you had some, but I should hate to hear about them—I am quite jealous enough for that. And if I had found another woman interesting, years ago, I don't think it would make you any happier to hear about it."

"You think it's best just to put a line through one's past?"

"Without any question. Only don't make it sound quite

so lurid, Gwyn. I feel that nothing you or I are likely to have done quite merits the dramatic word 'past'."

She was silent, and he glanced at her again, penetratingly, but not without a hint of amusement.

"My little girl, are you really so troubled about this?"

Her mouth quivered slightly, because it was unusual for him to be so tender with her. She nodded.

"But there is not the slightest need. If you want my perfectly serious view, it is that even two people who love each other and marry have a right to some private thoughts and memories of their own. That's sound sense, my dear, as well as sound morality. In theory, I know some other man has probably kissed you before I did, but I can bear it. In practice, I should probably want to wring his neck if I knew who it was."

She wondered fascinatedly what he would want to do to a man with whom she had slept, and to whom she had borne a child. But she didn't interrupt him.

"It's enough for me that I know you're dear and sweet and decent. Within that framework, it's hardly my business what you did before I knew you. And I'm perfectly willing to expound my view to the aunt herself, if that would satisfy you," he added with a touch of grim amusement again.

She knew that here was her opportunity to say—what about the things which might happen *outside* the framework of sweetness and decency, but the words simply wouldn't come.

With a quick movement, which she knew he would take for relief, she buried her face against him and held him very tightly. From his muttered exclamation she could tell he was unusually touched. She supposed it must seem strange and moving to him that his cool, self-confident fiancée should suddenly behave like this.

"Is it all right now?" his voice asked quietly, just above her head.

"Yes," Gwyneth whispered, and she could not have said herself whether her sigh was relieved or despairing.

She couldn't tell him. She *couldn't!* It would mean losing him, beyond question. The way he had spoken—lightly, but meaning it—of how he would feel towards a man who had only kissed her! No, she couldn't tell him. She couldn't alter things. They had stood like this for five years. It was too late to alter them now. She didn't want to use the calm, hateful, selfish arguments which Mother advanced, but they were true—they were true.

"Anyway, it isn't arguments that have convinced me," Gwyneth told herself with ruthless determination to face the truth. "It's simply that I can't bear to lose Van. It may be selfish and heartless, or it may be common sense and all for the best—but I'm not really working that out in my heart, I know. I only know that I can't lose Van."

With a tremendous effort, she regained her normal expression and looked up to smile at him. He was relieved, she saw and—not for the first time—she was struck by the strangeness of the fact that sometimes her slightest change of mood could affect him deeply.

In business, he was known as a stern, even a hard man, very difficult to move from any stand which he took up. She had once heard someone say of him dryly: "Steel is the right medium for Evander Onslie to deal in. It's like himself—clean and cold and unbreakable."

But when he was with her there was something warmer and more pliable about him. Only one was aware that, beneath the surface of his personal tenderness, there was that steely strength which his friends valued and his enemies feared.

"And now there are no more doubts?" he suggested, keeping his arm round her as they strolled on through the shrubbery.

"No, none at all." Gwyneth made that sound cool and confident again. She was beginning to re-adjust her mask once more—though oh, how she hated to have to wear it! For a little while she had supposed that the past was really dead and buried. It was living again now—living in a very real sense. She could only pretend it was not there. But it *was* there, all the same.

That night, when she was almost ready for bed, her mother came and knocked on her door.

"Gwyneth, may I come in?"

She hesitated, and then said:

"Yes, if you want to."

The last person she really wanted to see was her mother,

but she supposed it was only natural that some sort of discussion should take place.

Gwyneth had been seated at her dressing-table, and she turned now, with her arm over the back of the chair, her thick, bright hair falling forward a little over her forehead.

Mrs. Vilner didn't bother to sit down. She just asked baldly:

"Well, what did you tell him?"

"Nothing." Gwyneth said, just as curtly.

"Nothing?"

Gwyneth shook her head, and her mother gave a short, relieved laugh.

"You have more sense than I thought, Gwyneth."

"Or less conscience."

"It's the same thing," her mother replied cynically, and Gwyneth wondered again how her father had come to marry this strange and rather terrible woman.

"So you have decided, on balance, that what I did was right?" Mrs. Vilner said slowly. "I'm not perhaps so hateful and wicked, after all."

"I haven't worked out whether it's right or not," Gwyneth told her coldly. "In fact, I'm probably being weak and selfish. But I—love Van. I can't give him up, and it would mean doing that if—if he ever knew."

"It most certainly would. It is too much to ask any man to stand for—even a much more tolerant man than he is. If you want a child so much, I expect you and he will have one. You'd better leave it at that, and forget what is so much better forgotten. Good night, child." And her mother went out of the room.

Gwyneth looked after her for a moment, thinking how weirdly their conversation contrasted with the conversations which prospective brides were popularly supposed to have with their mothers.

She wished her mother had not said that last thing—about having a child by Van and forgetting whatever had gone before. It was fanciful, perhaps, but somehow those words seemed the last base piece of disloyalty to the poor unwanted little boy who was to be definitely shut out of everything.

"Am I really a very wicked woman?" thought Gwyneth, with a slight shiver. And the dark blue eyes which looked back at her from the mirror only asked the question again without answering it.

On the day of the wedding, weeks of fine weather broke in a violent thunderstorm.

While her mother and aunt spoke bitterly of the nuisance, and her father of his belief that it would clear up at any moment, Gwyneth thought: "How strange, there's always a storm on the important days of my life. If I were superstitious I should think it was unlucky."

But she was not superstitious, and she refused to think it was unlucky. She was marrying Van today and nothing else—or practically nothing else—mattered.

She was singularly unvain about her appearance in the ordinary way, but she knew she looked utterly beautiful in her wedding dress. Excitement had made her eyes very bright and her lips a deep, soft red. The faint, pinky glow of her dress seemed to repeat itself in the faint pink glow in her cheeks, and through the soft cloud of her veil gleamed her bright gold-brown hair.

As she came up the aisle on her father's arm, Van turned to watch her coming. He was completely at ease, cool and unperturbed by the people who stared at him, only waiting for her with a confident little smile of happiness that lightened his dark face indescribably.

Gwyneth had been extremely serious until then, but as her eyes met his, she smiled too. He looked so happy! What she was doing *was* right. To have killed so much happiness—and for what?—would have been stupid and cruel.

The voices of the choir soared upwards, clearly and sweetly. Distant thunder muttered a strangely effective accompaniment. In sonorous tones the Bishop demanded that anyone who knew just cause why they should not be joined together in holy matrimony should speak, or else (blessed words!) forever hold their peace.

In the deepest chamber of her memory, Gwyneth heard again a faint, childish wailing at those words. Then the fanciful moment passed. Van's ring was on her finger—bright, slender, infinitely dear.

She was his wife.

Afterwards, nearly everyone she had ever known came crowding round her. They wished her well, they compli-

mented her on her appearance, they kissed her and con-
gratulated her. It was all very charming and gay.

Gwyneth listened to the steady, murmured chorus of
approval, and was glad to see that it made her father very
happy indeed. Yes—again she could tell herself with certainty, she had been right to do what she had done.

"You looked beautiful, darling." Her mother, always
studiedly affectionate to her in public, smiled approval
upon her, and Gwyneth smiled back at her with the
requisite amount of daughterly feeling.

But it was at that moment that she was conscious of
being extraordinarily tired and wishing she could be alone
with Van.

At least twenty people told Gwyneth it was the nicest
wedding they remembered, and one added:

"There's something so natural and straightforward and
happy about your story, Gwyneth. No upsets or crises or
complications. Just a charming only daughter falling in
love and getting married and living happily ever after."

Gwyneth acknowledged that with a smile and some
pretty, conventional speech. But she took great care not to
meet her mother's eyes at that moment.

If they could have known! If they could have known!

But they didn't know. No one knew. That was what
made it possible to go on.

It was over at last. The last good wish had been expressed, the last good-bye said, and she and Van were
alone in the car on their way to London, where they were
to spend the night. The following day they were to fly over
to Switzerland for the ten days' honeymoon which was all
Van could allow himself from the business just now. But
in between came these few hours' interval, for which they
had made no plans and about which they felt deliciously
free.

The thunderstorm had cleared the air, and now the late
afternoon sunshine shed a soft, clear light on the surround-
ing country. The heavy stillness which had preceded the
storm had gone, and there was the almost imperceptible
but ceaseless movement of nature again.

Trees moved their branches and the leaves whispered together, the grass bent once more before the faintest breeze,

the birds twittered and sang and quarrelled, and occasionally a venturesome rabbit scurried through the hedge.

"It's heavenly, Van, isn't it?" she said impulsively.

He smiled.

"To have it all over, you mean?"

"Well—yes, that, too. I meant, really, that it's a wonderful evening, and it's good just to be alone together again."

"It's always good to be alone together," he assured her.

"Yes, of course." She leant back in her seat again and, taking off her hat, let the breeze stir the thick waves of her bright hair. "Were you nervous, Van?"

"At the wedding? Not in the least. Nor were you, were you?"

"No," Gwyneth said, and laughed slightly. "We weren't at all in character, were we? I ought to have whispered my responses shyly, and you ought to have fumbled with the ring and looked hot."

"Wouldn't you have hated that?"

"Yes, I should."

"And I should have hated it if you hadn't been cool and self-possessed. Your poise is one of the things I love about you." He said that almost casually, but she knew how deeply he meant it.

"I wasn't always like that, you know." She spoke reminiscently. "Cool and self-possessed, I mean. At seventeen I think I was unusually ingenuous and—shy."

"At seventeen one often is, I imagine."

"Were you?"

He laughed then with real amusement.

"Gwyneth dear, does it seem at all possible to you that I was ever ingenuous or shy?"

"No," Gwyneth had to admit, "it doesn't. And yet you must have been unsure of yourself once."

"I can't remember it," he confessed.

"Not as a child?"

Though he was looking ahead and smiling, he seemed to give that his serious attention.

"Sorry, Gwyneth. I was a self-sufficient little animal even then, I think. But I believe only children often are."

"I was an only child, but I was horribly dependent on other people's opinions and approval."

"And what changed you?"

38

That was spoken quite lightly, but she felt her throat contract at the thought of what *had* changed her.

"I just—grew up, I suppose," she said after a slight pause, but her tone was suddenly strangely hard and indifferent.

"Which means that you had a rotten experience you would rather forget."

"Van!" The coolness of that took her breath away. "What makes you think that?" she asked in a rather small voice.

"The tone of your voice, my dear, and a little elementary psychology. Besides, I always knew it."

"What do you mean? Always knew it?"

"The first time I saw you."

"It isn't possible!"

"Oh yes. You were talking to young Courtenay. Or rather, he was talking to you—trying to intrigue you and fascinate you. You were perfectly polite and charming to him, but he never even touched the fringe of the real you. You were thinking "I've heard all this before, and I've found it bitterly hollow." And then I knew that if I were to win you, I should have to start from something entirely different. The usual light, romantic stuff was not for you. You wanted something—stark and convincing."

"Do you mean that, even before you had spoken to me, you had ideas of—winning me—marrying me—whatever you like to call it."

"I like to call it "marrying"," he said with that dry little smile that was so very charming. "In that respect I am old-fashioned."

"Well, of course."

"I was terribly afraid that your detached air and your lack of interest in what Courtenay was saying meant that you *were* married already—unhappily married."

There was a short silence, and then, because she couldn't possibly leave things there, she said fascinatedly:

"And when you found I was not married, what did you think then?"

"That you must marry me."

"Yes, but—apart from that. I mean, what—what did you think was the matter?"

Glancing at him, she saw that his mouth had gone unusually gentle.

"You needn't say 'yes' or 'no' Gwyn dear, but I suppose some bounder made you desperately fond of him in the day when you were—what was it?—ingenuous and shy, and then let you down brutally—jilted you."

So that was what he thought! How innocent—how *trivial,* compared to the real truth!

"It was something like that," she heard herself say calmly. "But it's all over, long ago."

"He doesn't matter in the least now?"

"Matter? No, Van. He couldn't matter less," she exclaimed so passionately that he gave a peculiarly satisfied little smile. Then his expression became grave again, and he said with unusual gentleness:

"And I hope it doesn't hurt any more, my darling."

She felt the sudden tears come into her eyes.

"Nothing hurts when I have you," she told him slowly, and with a slight exclamation, he stopped the car and took her in his arms.

"Never think of it again, Gwyn. Promise me—for your own sake, as well as mine."

"I—promise. Of course I promise," Gwyneth said. And somehow that seemed even more irrevocable than the Bishop marrying them.

It was seven o'clock by the time they reached London, and after dinner in the great hotel restaurant, with its full-length windows opening on to the Park, they decided to go to the ballet.

She knew that the performance that evening was good, even without going into the finer points that might have delighted an expert, but she took in very little of it with her conscious mind. She was so keenly aware of Van beside her, and through her mind there ran like a happy refrain: "I'm married to Van. I am his wife. He loves me. It must be all right."

Their ten days' honeymoon was idyllically happy.

From the first moment, when the plane took off, Gwyneth had the feeling of literally soaring away, free, into the future. Her worries and her fears were left behind. The world was hers once more, as it had been when she was a schoolgirl.

They spent most of the time in Italian Switzerland, idling away long, sun-filled days on the lakes, fascinated by the beauty around them, almost drugged by the colour and the sunshine and the scent of flowers. Van had been there before, but for Gwyneth it was her first visit, and her pleasure doubled his.

At the hotel they were just one married couple among several. Their extreme self-possession suggested no necessity for 'honeymoon suites' or discreet solitariness. But to Gwyneth every hour had the hallmark of gold, the seal of pure happiness.

It was with real sadness that Gwyneth saw the last hours of her honeymoon slip away. But when they were actually on their way back to England, the thrill of going home—to a home which really was her own—wiped out anything else.

In the weeks before her marriage she had already spent a good deal of time supervising the furnishing of the very beautiful mansion flat overlooking the Park. Van had allowed her an entirely free hand in the matter, and the result was a home which was artistically perfect and personally dear. There had never been anything in Gwyneth's life to make her feel like that before. Even her own room at home had been subject to the decided, unmistakable hand of her mother. And when, now, the smiling new maid opened the door to them, Gwyneth, for all her self-possessed answering smile, was really thinking:

"This is my home—the centre of my new and wonderful life."

Almost immediately Van was caught up again in the network of his business life, and for the first few days she saw alarmingly little of him. He explained briefly that he had been away too long, and there were several things to bring up to date. After that he made no more apologies, and she had to make the best of his absence.

She imagined he scarcely spared a thought for her—but she found she was wrong. At the end of a week he came in one afternoon to find her having tea by herself in the green and cream lounge.

"You're early, Van." She glanced up and smiled at him.

"Yes." He came and leant his arms on the back of her chair and looked down at her. He didn't kiss her at first—

41

just watched her with an air of pleasure that softened his rather forbidding expression.

She went on pouring out tea.

"Aren't you going to sit down and have your tea?"

"In a minute. How lovely you are, Gwyn. It is wonderful to come home after a hell of a day and find you sitting here, as cool and lovely as ever, calmly pouring out tea."

She laughed—a soft, pleased little laugh, and leant back suddenly so that her hair brushed his hand.

"It's lovely to have you come in to tea—particularly as it's something of a novelty."

He bent and lightly kissed her cheek and then, rather unexpectedly, the side of her neck.

"I know. I'm quite aware that I've been a neglectful husband this last week. I couldn't help it, love. It will be better in future. Thank you for not making any trouble."

She put up her hand and touched his cheek.

"All right, Van."

That was all. But it was so strange and sweet to have him call her anything like that that she could have sung aloud.

He took his tea then, and presently asked her, with the air of a man who finds he has time to look round again and can now make plans to please himself:

"Are you free all day on Saturday?"

"Of course—if you want me."

"I always want you," he told her with a slight smile.

"Yes, but—Saturday? What are we going to do on Saturday?" She was aware of pleasurable anticipation.

"I want to go down to Greystones, the big orphanage in Hampshire, you know. I'm one of the chief trustees of the place—perhaps I told you before?" He paused a little interrogatively, and Gwyneth groped for words to reply.

"No," she said rather faintly, "I don't think you ever mentioned it."

"Well, I am. My father was, before me. He had a good deal to do with founding the place forty years ago, and I continued the connection with it. It's a wonderful place—an absolute model of its kind—and there have been one or two alterations which they want me to go down and see. The drive down is beautiful, and I thought it would be interesting for you, too. You have never seen it, I suppose?"

42

"No." She wondered if he, too, could hear by now how strange her voice sounded. "No, I've never seen it."

"And you would like to come with me?"

Terror and a sudden wild excitement seemed to envelop her in a sheet of flame. But she must answer calmly because, of course, he had asked a perfectly ordinary, undramatic question.

Very carefully she poured milk into her cup, taking care not to let her shaking hand rattle the jug against the cup.

"Yes, Van," she said considerably, "I think it would be very nice indeed. I'd like to go with you to—Greystones."

CHAPTER THREE

BETWEEN the decision to go and the arrival of Saturday morning, Gwyneth's spirits soared and sank in almost sickening alternation.

One moment, she knew she was mad not to make any sort of excuse for keeping away from the place and all the vague, unformed dangers it might represent. The next, she told herself that nothing dangerous could possibly result. Here indeed was the perfect opportunity for satisfying herself that the child—her child—was in happy surroundings.

"I shouldn't know him, of course," she kept on telling herself feverishly. "There's no way in which I *could* know. Only——" She never let herself get any further, but deep down in her heart was a strange, growing excitement. She knew it for something inexplicable and primitive—a queer, growing hunger to see the child she had believed to be dead for over five years.

And if she saw him—what then? If by some miracle she recognized him, knew him for her own?

But there was no answer to that question. She must hope it would never really arise.

Or must she? Could she even bear to go there and *not* know him?

And then she would start all over again.

Saturday was a day of perfect sunshine, so that the last excuse for postponing the visit disappeared. Van and she left London early, the big black car eating up the distance in a way that seemed to Gwyneth's excited nerves to sug-

43

gest that they were rushing madly towards some dramatic dénouement.

"I had a note from Dr. Kellaby this morning. He and his wife are expecting us to lunch and hope we will take enough time to see the place thoroughly," Van told her.

"Dr. Kellaby is the head of the place?"

"Yes. He's been Superintendent there for the last ten years. An excellent man for his job."

"Kind, you mean?"

"Oh, very, I should imagine. Exceedingly forceful and up-to-date in his views."

Van, of course, was considering him from the point of view of a trustee. She was considering him, she realized with a faint shock, from the point of view of a mother.

"He won't mind if I want to go round and see absolutely everything?" She wondered if that sounded like the reasonable interest of an ordinary visitor.

"I think both he and Mrs. Kellaby will be delighted."

"That's good. I—I'm really beginning to be awfully interested in the place."

It was not much more than half past eleven when they drove up to the picturesque grey stone building which represented 'home' to nearly a hundred children. It stood in several acres of very beautiful parkland, and Gwyneth thought with wistful eagerness: "He ought to be very happy here."

They were a little early, it seemed. Both Dr. and Mrs. Kellaby were still at a local committee meeting in connection with the arrangements for Founders' Day next month, but they would not be long. If Mr. and Mrs. Onslie would care to wait in the drawing room——?

They went through to the long drawingroom, where large french windows opened on to a very magnificent stretch of lawn. Groups of children were dotted about the green expanse, and someone in a nurse's uniform was sitting in a garden chair, knitting.

Almost immediately they were joined by an extremely alert-looking young man in horn-rimmed glasses, whom Van introduced as "Mr. Fothergill, the secretary and treasurer." He shook hands with Gwyneth, made an affable comment or two about the weather, and then engaged Van in an earnest conversation in which running expenses,

44

overhead charges and capital expenditure seemed to play about equal parts.

Gwyneth was not interested. She had not come down here to hear figures discussed. She wanted to go nearer to the children out there on the lawn—look at them for herself.

Turning to the two men, she said:

"Don't stop your discussion for me—but I'm going out on to the lawn. I want—I want to watch the children playing."

She smiled very charmingly at Mr. Fothergill and nodded casually to Van. Then, stepping out on to the terrace, she strolled across the lawn to where a group of the younger children were playing.

Van would think she was mildly interested in them, possibly even reflect: "Of course, the younger ones are always the most amusing to visitors."

That was what she was—just a visitor, with a passing interest in the younger children at the orphanage.

She stood a little way off from a small group, watching them playing, feeling strangely alien and lonely. One of those children might easily be her own, but she could not find words even to speak to them. It frightened her, and yet it excited her to watch them, and she could not tear herself away.

Which of those children was hers? Which—which—which? In a sense, it was not even her business, of course —but her blue eyes went searchingly from one little face to another, while her heart beat heavily and slowly.

The child with the smooth bright hair not unlike her own?—or perhaps that likeness was imagined. The dark, slightly aggressive one who insisted on the others doing what he wanted? That would be like Terry—dark, and slightly aggressive about his personal wishes. But again that likeness was probably the purest imagination. Her child might just as well be that pale, self-effacing little fellow in the green smock, or the tall, lanky child who seemed to have no special interest in anything or anyone, or the picture-book child who was trying to stand on his head.

Yes, that was the kind of child that every mother hoped her baby would be. Tight, golden curls, round pink cheeks, chubby legs and arms, laughing blue eyes—he was almost too good to be true. Anyone would want to adopt him if they could see him now, planting his curly head on the grass and cautiously raising first one fat leg and then the other. Suppose *that* were her child, and someone else had the idea of adopting——

"I can do that, too," observed a gruff little voice immediately beside her, and Gwyneth looked down to see a quaint little creature in a blue jersey suit, gazing with ill-concealed envy at the beautiful acrobat.

"Can you?" Gwyneth said, rather shyly because she scarcely knew how one treated small children.

"Yes, I can."

"Show me, then," she suggested coaxingly.

With great gravity and much puffing he proceeded to demonstrate very clearly that he could not. When he had fallen over several times, he rose to his feet once more, slowly dusting his hands together, and said:

"I can do it when people aren't looking."

"Can you really? Yes, I expect you can. I can do things best when people aren't looking," Gwyneth told him, carefully concealing her amusement.

"Can you stand on your head when people aren't looking?"

"Not very well," Gwyneth confessed. And then she sat down on the grass, because it was easier to talk to her little companion that way.

"I can't stand on my head, either," he admitted, and, sat down on the grass too. "And Freddie can't really stand on his head," he added, brushing his hand backwards and forwards across the daisies with elaborate casualness. "He can only put his head down and *one* foot up."

It was all too true.

Gwyneth glanced once more at the beautiful Freddie. He was the right way up now, and even more beautiful that way. Again her heart beat heavily.

"How old is Freddie?" she asked abruptly, as though the child beside her was a grown-up.

"I don't know."

No, of course he wouldn't. He was too young to be really informative. She would have to ask someone else— and the time was already growing short, it seemed to her.

She glanced away across the lawn again, but Van and Mr. Fothergill were still deep in conversation.

"*I'm* five an' a half—nearly six," said the gruff little voice beside her.

Gwyneth's eyes came back to the child.

He was lying flat on his stomach now, not looking at her, but regarding a single daisy with the greatest attention. Something in his air told her at once what was the matter. He didn't want her to be interested in Freddie's age. He wanted her to be interested in *his* age.

"Are you? And what is your name?" That sounded rather like the classic old gentleman in funny stories, she thought, but the little boy seemed quite satisfied with this standard of conversation. He sat up at once and said:

"My name's Toby."

That made Gwyneth want to laugh, because somehow the name suited him absurdly well. In particular it suited the grave, abnormally deep voice that seemed to come out of the depths of his jersey.

He was not a specially pretty child, but his solemn eyes were a beautiful dark blue, and his hair turned back over the top of his head in a quaint 'quiff'.

"He's more like a mascot thán a hero," thought Gwyneth amusedly, and at that moment he said:

"Do you like it?"

"What, dear?"

"Do you like my name?" He was evidently a bit crest-fallen and she saw she was doing badly.

"It's a lovely name," Gwyneth told him hastily. "I've never known another Toby."

"No. There isn't one," he explained simply. She realized then that in his world, limited by the orphanage, there *wasn't* another Toby, and therefore he knew himself to be unique.

"I have a little china jug at home called Toby. Would you like to have it?" Gwyneth said suddenly. She could not exactly explain the impulse which prompted the offer. The jug was quite a lovely miniature specimen, now she came to remember it. But the astounded pleasure on the child's face intrigued her immensely.

He came nearer to her.

"Do you mean—keep it?"

47

Gwyneth nodded, her smiling eyes on his face.

"A little jug—and it's called Toby," he repeated slowly and with great pleasure. "We've got a big jug that holds all our milk, but it hasn't got a name."

"No—this is a very special jug," Gwyneth explained. "It has a man's face on it."

"What man?"

"Well——" She was rather nonplussed. "He's Toby, too, I suppose."

"Toby Two? And I'm Toby One." This pleased the little boy immensely, and he rolled on the grass and chortled with joy.

Gwyneth had no experience of the odd things that a child will find funny, and she was very much intrigued by this display. She was laughing a good deal, too, over the absurdity of it when a shadow fell across her, and, glancing up, she saw that Van was standing looking down at her, smiling slightly at her pleasure.

"Oh, did you want me?"

"Well, I think the Kellabys are just due back now, and we shall be expected to go round and admire the extension to the Infants' Dormitory."

"Of course," Gwyneth stood up at once. She might be able to glean a few scraps of information, ask a few innocent questions. One never knew.

"Oh, are you going?" Toby got to his feet, too, looking very disappointed.

"Well, I'm going to see the new dormitory," Gwyneth explained.

"I'll show you," he offered pressingly, but she felt bound to veto that.

"I think Mr. Kellaby wants to show me. But I'll come back to speak to you before I go, and I won't forget to send you the Toby jug." She smiled at him as she turned away with Van.

But she had not gone more than a dozen steps before—

"I'm coming, too," observed the gruff little voice conversationally—and there he was, trotting along beside her, trying hard to keep pace with her and Van.

Van glanced down from his great height.

"Who is your bass-baritone friend?" he asked her.

"His name is Toby."

"Toby One," came in deep tones, slightly to the rear of them now.

"Van"—she slackened her pace—"we'll have to go more slowly. He can't keep up with us."

"Is he supposed to be keeping up with us?" Van asked, but he, too, slowed his footsteps. "Look here, young man"—he addressed himself to their shadow—"you run along and play with the others over there."

Toby flung a disparaging glance at the group now some way behind.

"I don't want to play," he stated. "I want to come, too."

"But I don't think you can come with us."

Toby stood on one foot and swung the other backwards and forwards at a perilous angle.

"I'm not coming with you," he said. "I'm coming with her."

The subtle flattery was not wasted. Gwyneth felt herself begin to weaken badly.

"Perhaps he could come with us, Van. It's not like an official inspection."

Van looked at Toby. He was not used to individual children—was, in fact, much more at home as the trustee of many than the companion of one. But the little creature, with its dogged determination and its odd deep voice, was difficult to resist.

"We'll see what Kellaby says," he compromised, and Gwyneth and Toby took this for permission. She held out her hand, which Toby grasped firmly.

Rather more slowly they made their way towards the house, from which Dr. Kellaby, accompanied by his wife, could now be seen emerging.

"I'm so sorry we weren't here when you arrived, but I hope Fothergill made our excuses." Dr. Kellaby, a pleasant, authoritative man in his early fifties, greeted them both cordially, while Mrs. Kellaby told Gwyneth how very pleased they were that she had come down to see the orphanage so soon after her marriage.

For some reason, no one seemed to notice Toby particularly, and almost immediately Dr. Kellaby suggested that they should begin by inspecting the new Infants' Dormitory. They strolled towards the house, Dr. Kellaby explaining as they went:

"The old one was completely redecorated, of course, and is now given over entirely to the over-sevens. Much more suitable for them. But, so far as the new one is concerned——" He plunged into detail, and it was evident that the whole matter was very dear to his heart. Van commented and asked questions in a way which showed he had followed the progress of the building very closely and interestedly, too.

Gwyneth, meanwhile, made conversation with Mrs. Kellaby who walked in step with her, but on the side away from Toby. It gave Gwyneth a pleasant feeling of conspiracy when anxious little fingers pressed into hers, to indicate satisfaction that so far they were safe. He took it so completely for granted that she was as eager as he, that he should be included in the party.

Just as they reached the entrance, Dr. Kellaby turned to say something to her, and noticed that Toby was still firmly attached to them.

"Here, young man," he said, just as Van had, "you run along and find the others. You ought to be out playing in the sunshine."

This was the voice of recognized authority, and everyone looked at Toby. He wilted slightly in the full glare of publicity. Then he looked at Gwyneth, and Gwyneth looked at Van.

"I believe," Van said in that grave, rather stern way of his, "that—er—Toby is helping to conduct this tour of inspection. He was going to explain one or two things to my wife."

"Is that so?" The Superintendent looked amused. "But I think——"

"Please, Dr. Kellaby, may he come too? I—we're getting on so well," Gwyneth said, "and it's nice to hear what one of the children has to say about the place."

He hadn't really had anything to say about the place—or its inmates—of course (apart from the observation that Freddie couldn't stand upon his head) but Dr. Kellaby accepted the suggestion with a smile, and the party, including Toby, moved into the house.

"Actually, Toby is rather a favourite of my husband, too," Mrs. Kellaby explained in a tone inaudible to the little boy. "He is the only one of all our children who comes from north of the Tweed, and, as I expect you can hear, my husband is Scottish, too." She laughed agreeably, and somehow Gwyneth managed to laugh too.

What did she mean, this pleasant, placid woman, who had no idea she was saying anything significant? That Toby came of Scottish parents? That he had been born in Scotland (*the only one*) and then brought south?

She must say something and say it quickly or the subject would be changed and the moment lost. Even as Mrs. Kellaby began a comment on the size of the new dormitory, Gwyneth cut across the sentence with an eagerness she could not wholly hide.

"Were his—people Scottish?"

"My husband? Yes. They came from——"

"No. The little boy's."

"Oh." Mrs. Kellaby glanced at Toby who was still contentedly clinging to Gwyneth's hand, unaware that he was being discussed. "I don't really know, because it's one of the strict rules of the place that only my husband knows the full circumstances of each case—so far as the relations disclose them, of course."

"Yes, of course. But your husband—he did say that the child was Scottish? I mean, what made you think he was?"

Mrs. Kellaby laughed.

"I always remember my husband coming in just after Toby had been brought here, and saying: "Well, we've got a real little Scottie this time. Straight from the Highlands, and no more than a week or two old." He was quite delighted. Toby was the youngest child we ever had, I should think, and even then he had been in a Scottish children's hospital first, I believe. Possibly the mother died when he was born. I don't know."

"You mean she couldn't have been so—so heartless as to—part with him otherwise?"

"Oh, I don't know about that. Circumstances can be very cruel. It's hard for us even to imagine what lies behind some of these cases, you know, Mrs. Onslie—and it certainly isn't for us to judge," the Superintendent's wife said kindly. And something in the tolerant humanity of that calmed Gwyneth just a little.

She was silent, pretending to pause for a moment to look at the view from one of the windows, pretending to take

51

the deepest interest in the fire-proof staircase and panelling on the way upstairs. And all the while, clutching her hand —swinging it lightheartedly at times—was Toby, her own child.

Gwyneth hardly dared to look at him. To feel his small fingers was enough. She tried to tell herself that she might be jumping to conclusions too quickly, the the evidence was, to say the least of it, scrappy.

That was all true, but it made no difference. She knew now that Toby was hers. She was not interested any more in any hypothetical little boy—not even if he were as beautiful as Freddie and the admiration of all. She wanted this dear, odd little creature with the gruff voice and the dark blue eyes and the rather absurd hair. She *wanted* him —that was the awful part.

Her eyes went then to Van, grave, thoughtful, absorbed in what Dr. Kellaby was saying to him. Van!—who was entirely unaware of the drama that was being played out beside him, whose complete world would crash in ruins if she said, in effect: "This child holding on to my hand is really my own. I must take him away with me."

No—it was impossible. You couldn't ask a man who was trustee of an orphanage suddenly to swallow the fact that one of the orphans was the illegitimate child of his own wife.

Her head began to swim, and with an effort she pulled herself together again.

And then Dr. Kellaby—Mrs. Kellaby—what would they think? Not that it really mattered, of course, beside this frantic, growing desire to pick up Toby and take him away with her. But they *were* part of the problem. They represented the outside world.

"Look," Toby said importantly at that moment. "There's *my* bed. That's where I sleep."

Until then Gwyneth had hardly realized that they were in the much discussed new dormitory. Now she looked with overwhelming interest at the bed where her little boy slept.

"It's a very nice bed," Toby informed her, and bounced upon it to demonstrate the fact. But a firm word from Dr. Kellaby put an end to that, and he got off it again rather meekly.

"That table's half mine." He showed her a small table which stood between his bed and the next one.

52

"Is it?"

"Yes. I shall put Toby Two there."

She saw he had by no means forgotten the promised present, and she supposed with a little wrench at her heart that orphans could not, in the nature of things, have many presents. She thought of the toys and clothes she would love to give him, the miniature furniture that would delight him and make him give his funny, deep chuckle.

It was incredible—but *she could not give him those things!* She would have to go away presently, like any other visitor, and apparently not think of him again—except to send him her Toby jug as a pleasant memento from a casual caller who happened to be amused by his name.

"I can't bear it!" thought Gwyneth. "I simply can't bear it!"

But she had to, of course, like everything else connected with this unhappy secret. She even had to bear it when a big bell rang and Mrs. Kellaby said:

"That's lunch-time for you, Toby. Say good-bye to Mrs. Onslie and run along to the dining-room now."

He didn't really want to go, but the call of food was enticing, and his counter-proposals were more half-hearted this time. It was Gwyneth who wanted to say:

"Let him stay with me—please let him stay with me. I want to see him eat his lunch. Can't he have it with us?"

But of course it was quite impossible to say such things. She had to pat his head and let him go. She couldn't even kiss him because she was not sure if visitors did kiss the children, or whether it was considered unhygienic or something of the sort. She mustn't do anything the least bit noticeable—not even anything that might strike Van as emotional and unlike her.

The only thing she could do was to call after the little figure trotting out of the dormitory:

"I'll see you again before I go, Toby."

And Toby replied: "Yes, I'll see you too."

"He's quaint, isn't he?" Mrs. Kellaby said with a laugh when he had gone. "He practically never says just "yes" or "no", but always a whole sentence."

"He's sweet," Gwyneth agreed as casually as she could. "How old is he?"

"Going on for six. I think he has a birthday in September." Gwyneth had known it would be so, of course, but she listened fascinatedly to this further confirmation. Mrs. Kellaby turned to her husband. "Toby is one of the Septembers, isn't he?"

Dr. Kellaby smiled.

"Yes. He seems to have taken a fancy to you, Mrs. Onslie."

"I was very flattered. He's a dear child. The kind—the kind of child one could get very fond of. Don't you think so, Van?"

Her husband looked rather surprised, smiled slightly and said:

"Yes, I dare say. Funny little beggar." And then he began to talk to Dr. Kellaby again about Annual Meetings and other uninteresting things.

Gwyneth didn't enjoy the rest of her visit very much. It was hard to show a practical and intelligent interest in the things which didn't concern her own child very personally.

It was hard to have to make casual conversation over lunch, too. She wanted to say:

"When can I see Toby again? Can I have an hour with him all by myself before I go? Could I have him stay with me? Do people ever adopt the children from here?"

But she couldn't ask these questions—not one of them. They would all sound extraordinary—and whatever she did, she must not arouse suspicion.

The afternoon dragged away. She had seen everything by the end—the schoolrooms, the play-rooms, the kitchens, the grounds—and she had expressed a proper interest in them all. Only at the very end, when they were within ten minutes of going, did she pluck up courage to say:

"I haven't seen Toby to say good-bye."

"Toby?" Her husband looked surprised. "Do you want to see the child again?"

"I promised him I would. I couldn't think of letting him down," Gwyneth said almost sharply.

"A very good rule, Mrs. Onslie," Dr. Kellaby agreed with a smile. "Children notice promises at least as much as grown-ups."

"Of course, if you promised him." Van smiled slightly, too. "I didn't realize that a promise was involved."

So Toby was summoned, and Gwyneth had to say good-bye to him in front of them all. It didn't count as seeing him at all, of course. She couldn't kiss him and hug him, as she wanted. She could only take his little hand and smile upon him very sweetly and say:

"Good-bye, Toby. I won't forget to send you your jug."

But he was better at this sort of thing than she was. He held up his face to be kissed and said:

"Thank you. Good-bye. Please don't forget my jug."

Everyone smiled then, and so it was quite easy to bend down and kiss him. His mouth felt very soft and damp, and she thought: "He's only a baby—my baby."

"When shall I see you again?" he asked firmly.

"I—don't know." It made her want to cry, having to say that.

"I dare say Mrs. Onslie will be down here on Founders' Day," Mrs. Kellaby suggested pleasantly. And at that, Gwyneth could have fallen on her neck and kissed her.

"Yes—yes, of course. When is it?" She had not dared to think of some possibility like that.

"In about six weeks' time."

"Near my birthday," supplemented Toby innocently.

"I'll come. It's a promise," Gwyneth assured him, trying not to notice that Van's eyes were on her in rather amused surprise.

And, after that, they said their goodbyes to the Kellabys and went away.

At first they drove in silence. Then presently Van said: "It's a fine place, isn't it?"

"Yes. Wonderful. I can quite understand your interest in it."

"I wondered once or twice if you had had more than enough."

"Oh no. Really, Van, no!" She was desperately anxious to show any amount of interest that might mean their going back again.

Her vehemence seemed to amuse him slightly.

"You don't have to be interested just because I am," he told her reassuringly. "But I expect you were more interested in the personal side—the children themselves rather than in the first-class organization."

"Yes, I was. That—that little boy who was so friendly— I thought he was sweet."

"Yes. A nice child. I'm afraid I'm not much good at patting their little heads and making conversation. The business side of the place is more in my line than personal contacts."

"I didn't imagine *I* knew much about what to say to children, but he was quite easy."

Her husband nodded carelessly.

"Van, I like him so much." She tried to make that sound like any woman who just happened to be intrigued by the child. "I wonder if I could have him home?"

Van looked simply astounded.

"For the day, do you mean? I shouldn't think so, my dear. I imagine that sort of thing would be very unsettling for an institution child. I am sure the Kellabys wouldn't encourage it."

She knew he didn't mean it at all unkindly, but to hear her little boy described as 'an institution child' set her teeth on edge.

"You—you could use a certain amount of influence, I suppose?"

"I could, Gwyneth," he said a trifle dryly, "but I don't think I should. The child is probably very well where he is, and in our particular position, we are scarcely the people who ought to start agitating for rules to be broken."

She was silent, not because she thought—as he evidently did—that the discussion was ended, but because she was thinking how to approach it in a different way.

"Van, we shall go down there again on Founders' Day, shan't we?"

"Certainly, if you would like to. I almost always go. And I'm sure they would take it as a pleasant compliment if you came, too."

"I should like to."

There was silence again for a while and, glancing at him, she felt sure that his thoughts were now on something else —probably business affairs, since their drawing near London would bring those to his mind. She must speak to him again, before he was quite detached from his profound, if impersonal, interests in Greystones.

"Van."

"Um-hm?"

"If I spoke very tactfully to Mrs. Kellaby on Founders'

56

Day, and found out whether we *could* have——have Toby for a visit, would you have any personal objection? I mean, if *they* don't object?"

Van slowed the car and looked at her in surprise.

"My dear girl, are you seriously suggesting the child should *stay* with us?"

"Yes." She hoped he wouldn't hear that she spoke with the obstinacy of despair.

"Why, Gwyneth, I think that's a little too impulsive a decision, don't you?"

"It isn't a decision exactly. I—I just wanted to discuss it and see how you liked the idea."

There was a pause, then he said dryly and flatly:

"I don't like it at all?"

"Oh, Van, why?"

"My dear, we've only been married a few weeks—only had our home to ourselves for about ten days. Decidedly, I don't want a child running about the place."

She didn't answer, and perhaps he got the impression that she resented his saying that. He flushed rather deeply, an extremely unusual thing with him.

"Well," he said slowly, "I'll amplify that to what I really mean. I don't specially want a child about the place unless it's my child."

He couldn't possibly know, of course, how terribly significant his way of putting it seemed to her. He had said '*my* child'—not 'your child' or even 'our child'. Somehow his choice of words seemed to shut a door against Toby.

There didn't seem anything else to say, but evidently her silence troubled him, because he stopped the car altogether, turning to face her with his arm along the back of the seat.

"Gwyneth, did you resent my saying that?"

"About not wanting Toby, you mean?"

"No." He dismissed Toby again with very slight impatience. There was a short pause. Then he said with something of an effort: "Did you mind the implication that we might have a child of our own some time?"

"Van!—of course not." She realized then that, in her preoccupation with Toby, she had scarcely noticed Van's change of tone. She caught his hand eagerly, in an unusual access of emotion. "I hope we do have a child, my dear— every bit as much as you do."

57

That was true—she did hope it. Only that must not shut out Toby. It *must* not.

"Thank you, darling," Van said in that curt, almost formal way of his, and leaning forward, he kissed her on her lips.

It wasn't possible to start the subject of Toby again after that, however much she might long to. Besides, what Van had said about their having had their home to themselves for only ten days was true. It was unreasonable and unkind to expect him to contemplate an intruder, yet—even such a small intruder as Toby.

She tried to point out very reasonably to herself that she had managed very well without her child for five years. Why must she feel now that she could scarcely bear to pass a day without knowing what was happening to him?

Very common sense, of course. But it didn't alter the fact that, now she had *seen* him, everything was changed —just as everything had been changed that day long ago when she had first heard him crying.

The next few weeks were not altogether easy ones for Gwyneth. When Van was with her and they were doing the things which they had always loved to do together, it was all right. She was happy and she knew she made him happy.

But there were long hours when Van was away at the office. In the ordinary way, this would not have worried her. There was plenty for her to do—in her home and in the social circle to which Van Onslie's wife naturally had to belong. Only now, when Van was not there, her thoughts fled at once to the little boy at Greystones who was hers and yet not hers, and then they would go round and round the same weary circle again.

When could she tactfully mention the subject to Van once more? How would he take it? What could she say that would make him, too, want to have Toby, at any rate for a visit? If Toby then made his own appeal, what would Van think if she suggested adopting him? How could she best put it? How would he take it?

It was not possible to find the answers to these questions, nor was it possible to escape asking herself the same questions all over again.

Carefully packing up the little jug, she sent it to Toby

just a few days after the visit, and in reply she received a cordial letter from the matron, explaining that the jug had arrived safely and that Toby was extremely delighted with it. She read the letter many times and tried to imagine his pleasure when the parcel arrived. But it was all so remote when his baby enthusiasm had to be expressed in type-writing before she could hear about it.

Somehow she had supposed something might come of this incident, but, of course, it didn't. And silence closed down on Greystones again.

During the first week in September Mrs. Vilner stayed in London for a day or two on her way to Paris. Gwyneth spent some time shopping with her, and listened with her cool, remote smile to her mother's open congratulations on the excellent match she had made.

"I had a few doubts at one time, Gwyneth. Those successful, unsmiling business men sometimes make very hard husbands."

"Van has a very charming smile when he likes," protested Gwyneth mildly.

"Yes, yes. I know. But it is when *he* likes—not to please other people. However, it's easy to see he is thoroughly indulgent where you are concerned."

Gwyneth didn't think 'indulgent' was quite the word, but she let that pass.

"We're very happy," she said conventionally, and her mother laughed softly.

"All of which goes to show that I was right in what I did," she observed lightly.

Something in the complacency of that, infuriated Gwyneth. She shattered her mother's cool self-satisfaction with the one brutal remark:

"I went with Van to see Greystones a few weeks ago."

"You——' Mrs. Vilner stopped dead in the middle of Regent Street, and then went on again more slowly. It was very seldom indeed that she lost her composure, but this time there was no doubt of it.

"Did anything—unfortunate happen?" There was that hard thread in her beautiful voice which was only there when she was either very angry or very much disturbed.

"I saw my little boy, if you call that unfortunate."

Gwyneth extracted a sort of fierce pleasure from readministering some of the shocks which she herself had received.

"You mean you—knew him? But you couldn't!"

"He knew me," Gwyneth said slowly. And then suddenly she very much wanted to cry.

"He *knew* you? He couldn't know you. How do you mean? That he recognized you as his mother?"

"No, not that. He—he picked me out at once and wanted to stay near me. He insisted on coming with me and—and showing me things."

"Oh—*that*." Her mother gave an annoyed, relieved laugh. "Lots of children take a fancy to one person and follow them round."

"It wasn't that." Gwyneth's tone was cold yet fierce.

"How did you know it was—the child? What proof was there?"

Gwyneth began to wish now that she had never mentioned Toby to her mother. She was the last person, really, with whom she wanted to discuss things, and only the urge to speak to *someone* about him had moved her to say anything.

"It doesn't matter. We won't talk about it any more," she told her mother curtly.

The subject was only obliquely referred to again before Mrs. Vilner left, and that was hardly an occasion of her own making. She asked quite innocently:

"Gwyneth, where is your miniature Toby jug? I thought you meant to have it here, on this table."

"I did, but——" Gwyneth hesitated a second, and Van supplied the explanation.

"Gwyneth took a great fancy to one of the children down at Greystones. His name was Toby and she thought he would like the jug. I suppose he was interested in it when he heard about it."

"I—see."

Gwyneth refused to look in her mother's direction. She knew quite well that those rather cat-like eyes were thoughtfully on her, but not by so much as a glance would she add to her mother's knowledge.

Van spoke casually of something else, the moment passed—— And the next morning Mrs. Vilner left for Paris, still without having touched on the subject again.

CHAPTER FOUR

AFTER her mother's departure Gwyneth was conscious of an immediate lightening of her spirits. Breakfast alone with Van was twice as delightful as usual, and when he looked up from his post, he found her smiling slightly from sheer pleasure.

"Well?" He smiled, too, as he took his coffee from her hand.

"Nothing—except it's nice just to be by ourselves again."

He laughed then, and she knew he was pleased. And then she wondered if that would make him feel less inclined than ever to have Toby. She wished she could think of something clever and tactful to turn that around a little. But before she could think of anything, he addressed her instead.

"Could you find time to meet my young cousin Paula, one afternoon?"

"Of course, Paula? I don't seem to remember her at our wedding."

"No. She was away in Brussels at a finishing school at the time. She has only just come home."

"Oh—she's a lot younger than you?"

"Good heavens, yes! Much more like a niece than a cousin. In fact, most of my recollections of her centre round feeding her up with too much ice-cream on half-term holidays."

"But she is rather a favourite of yours?"

Again that slight smile showed.

"I have no favourites—except you." For a moment his dark eyes rested on her with extreme pleasure. "But she is a nice child. Gay and a little impertinent, but well-meaning and full of good spirits. Oddly enough, her parents are quite elderly people. They live in a large, gloomy house at Norbury."

"Oh, that isn't much fun for her, I should think," Gwyneth said with sympathy.

"No, that's how I feel about it. And while I deplore the phrasing of this appeal, I suppose I ought to do something about it." And rather amusedly he tossed over a sheet of thick cream notepaper, covered with large, round handwriting.

Van darling [Gwyneth read, with a certain amount of amused admiration for anyone who could address her forbidding husband in this extravagant style], do be an angel and come to my rescue! I'm awfully glad to be home from school and all that, but honestly, it's just about as lively as a morgue here. Daddy fixes chess and bowls as the very limit of riotous excitement, while Mother thinks an annual visit to a Shakespearean tragedy quite enough light entertainment for anyone.

I was thinking of taking to secret drinking or something of the sort to drown my sorrow and boredom—and then I thought of you. I know you've acquired a wife since I last saw you, but you must be getting a bit sick of each other by now. Wouldn't you like a nice, entertaining girl like myself to come along and amuse one or both of you?

Van, do take me out to something. You see, I'm quite shameless cadging, but what can a poor girl do? Anyway, the parents consider you old enough to be safe (forgive me if that adjective stings) and of course, as a married man you're doubly safe. Ask your wife if I may borrow you for once, will you? Thanks a lot. Paula.

Gwyneth put down the letter and laughed.

"But, my dear Van, it isn't me she wants to see. It's you."

"Oh, I dare say." Her husband brushed that aside with careless determination. "Schoolgirl crushes are not in my line."

"But it's so much more fun when you're nineteen to be taken out by a distinguished-looking man than by a mere female cousin by marriage," objected Gwyneth, with some sympathy for the outrageous Paula.

Van, however, was not to be drawn.

"No, no. I'll take you both to the theatre in the evening, if you like."

"Very well. Though she'll probably put me down as a poor possessive creature who dare not lend her husband to an innocent young relation."

But Van didn't think that sort of thing funny. He just frowned and said: "If she's such a damned fool as to say

62

so, she can go back to Norbury and play chess with her father."

"Poor kid," laughed Gwyneth. "Phone her and ask her if she would like to come shopping with me one afternoon. I'll bring her back here for dinner and we can go on to a show later."

"I will." Van pushed back his chair and got up. "I must go. It's later than I thought." He bent down to give her that apparently careless kiss for which she waited each morning with an ever-fresh thrill of pleasure. "There's our official invitation to Founders' Day at Greystones, by the way. I don't know if you still want to go."

"Van, of *course!*"

She somehow managed not to snatch at the handsomely printed invitation card, but to take it instead with a moderate show of pleasure and interest. And then he went off, leaving her with the card in her hand.

She read the printed words again and again. So formal—but they were her pass to a stolen paradise.

She was determined there should be no risk of their not accepting that invitation, and by the time Van came in that evening, she had already replied to it. He was a little amused and said rather teasingly:

"Is your gruff-voiced admirer responsible for this eagerness?"

"Toby?" She contrived to sound mildly amused. "I like to see all the children—but he is the special favourite."

Van nodded, but did not pursue the subject. Instead, he said:

"I rang up Paula, and she will be very delighted to go with you on Wednesday if that suits you. I'll get tickets for the new revue at the Corinthian. I suppose that's the sort of thing she will like."

"I should think so. Everyone says it's splendid. Is she coming here to meet me?"

"Yes. I'll come in to lunch that day if I can, but if not, I don't think she will find much difficulty in introducing herself."

Nor, judging from the letter, did Gwyneth. And when Wednesday came and Van had to go to a business lunch after all, Gwyneth awaited, with a certain amount of curiosity, the advent of Paula.

Her gay, fresh voice in the hall was quite a fitting announcement of her arrival, and when Gwyneth came forward to welcome her, she saw that the newly-acquired young cousin was an extremely pretty girl.

She was dressed in a vivid sunshine-yellow suit, which Gwyneth felt sure hailed from the Brussels rather than the Norbury part of Paula's existence, and on her curly dark head was perched a big yellow hat. She had great dark eyes —not unlike Van's, except that hers sparkled impudently while his were calm and usually a little stern—and her smile displayed the most perfect teeth Gwyneth had ever seen.

"How d'you do? You're Gwyneth, aren't you?"

Gwyneth's hand was grasped firmly, while she was subjected to the most frankly interested scrutiny.

"Yes. And you're Paula."

"The *enfant terrible* of our family," Paula agreed, not without a touch of youthful pride.

"Rather more *'enfant'* than *'terrible'*?" Gwyneth suggested with a smile. "Or do you regard that as an insult?"

Paula gave a surprised little laugh as she dropped down comfortably into a corner of the settee.

"Maybe it's true." She smiled at Gwyneth again with that undisguised interest. "I didn't expect you to be quite the sort to say that," she added candidly.

"No? What sort did you expect me to be?"

"Oh—aloof and correct and dignified."

"How horrid. What gave you that idea?"

"I thought that was the kind of wife Van would choose."

"Oh, come," Gwyneth laughed protestingly. "Do you think Van himself is so—what was it?—aloof and correct and dignified?"

"No-o. But one feels his slogan is "Only the best will do". I always expected that, having built up his big position, he'd suddenly think: "Dear me, what I want is a wife to crown this edifice"—and then he'd look round and select a Caesar's wife sort of person to pop on top."

"And, from your tone, I don't fill the bill?" Gwyneth suggested regretfully.

"You're much nicer," Paula said with such a frank smile of approval that Gwyneth's heart warmed to the absurd child in her stunning hat.

"She's terribly young," Gwyneth thought, "in spite of her confident air."

Apparently Paula was thinking the same of her because, pulling off the hat and ruffling up her hair, she remarked:

"I know it's not the thing to ask such questions, but you're lots younger than Van, aren't you?"

"I am younger," Gwyneth admitted.

"I'm so glad. It makes you so much easier to talk to." That was suddenly wistful rather than confident, and Gwyneth wondered curiously if Paula had the same doubts and problems which *she* had had at her age. Not quite such grim problems, of course, but the same feeling of insecurity.

She glanced at the pretty, rather clouded face opposite.

"What is it, Paula? Are you in need of someone to talk to, then?"

"Sometimes—frightfully."

"It isn't a bad thing to confide in one's parents." Gwyneth felt something of a hypocrite as she remembered the relationship between herself and her own parents, but she didn't want to encourage this charming, tiresome young creature to believe she was misunderstood at home.

"But there are some things you can't discuss with parents," Paula objected.

"Are there?"

"Oh dear—did you discuss everything with yours?"

There was a slight pause.

"No. To be quite truthful, I didn't. But then my mother and I were never very close together."

"I've not much in common with mine, either."

Gwyneth rose to her feet with some decision.

"Look here, my child, we're getting on rather doubtful ground. I may be very sympathetic and all that, but I'm not going to play the role of listener while you grumble about your parents. If we're going shopping, we had better go now."

"I wasn't grumbling," Paula assured her, as she got to her feet more slowly. "They're rather dears, as a matter of fact, my parents. Only they're very remote from anything I *feel*."

Something in that struck an answering chord in Gwyneth's heart. It *was* difficult when you couldn't find people who shared your feelings. On a most unusual impulse, she put her arm round the girl.

"Well, my dear, if you want to regard me as a suitable confidante, I'm very flattered. Perhaps I am near enough to your age to share your feelings better than an older person. Any time you want to use me as a safety valve, you're welcome to. Is that what you want me to say?"

"Yes. You're a darling, Gwyneth. No wonder Van adores you."

"How do you know he does?" Gwyneth laughed, but she flushed slightly, too.

"He said so."

"When?"

"In the letter he wrote in answer to my congratulations. At least, he said you were as near perfect as a woman could be without becoming uninteresting."

"He said—*that*?" There was pain as well as pleasure in Gwyneth's exclamation. She wondered with what imaginary virtues he endowed her when he ranked her so near perfection. It made one a little afraid.

She found Paula an excellent companion that afternoon —gay, sweet-tempered and amusing, and by common consent, they cut short the shopping and motored out down the river to have tea at some quiet spot where they could talk without interruption and get to know each other better.

"Do you always drive your own car?" Paula wanted to know.

"Usually. I drove a good deal before my marriage. We lived in the country, you know, and I had to. I got used to it."

Paula seemed to consider the general scheme of Gwyneth's life before she was married, and suddenly she came out with:

"You were a Canon's daughter, weren't you?"

"I was."

"Did you have to be awfully circumspect and well-behaved?"

A faintly bitter smile just touched Gwyneth's lips at that, but she suppressed it at once. The child couldn't know how ironical that was.

"I had to have some regard for appearances, if that's what you mean. But that isn't a bad thing, you know, Paula. Sometimes it keeps one from doing rather silly things."

(And sometimes it didn't, of course.)

Paula frowned slightly.

"I suppose you met Van in a very correct and conventional manner?"

Gwyneth raised her eyebrows slightly, and even Paula seemed to become aware that curiosity was outrunning good manners.

"I'm sorry, Gwyneth. Mustn't I say things like that? Only I really had a reason for asking."

"Had you? Well, I met Van at a perfectly conventional New Year party, if you must know. Why? Do you think it's more romantic to meet unconventionally?"

"Don't you?"

"No, I don't," Gwyneth said, with a painfully sharp remembrance of a sunlit glade and a romantic little fool listening to pleasant stuff about enchanted princesses.

"Oh dear! Are you very sticky about that sort of thing?"

"Meaning?" Gwyneth smiled a little at the disconsolate tone.

"Gwyneth, do you think it's—cheap, to get to know anyone without all the usual introductions and that sort of thing?"

"Well"—Gwyneth began to see the red light flickering—"it's a pretty safe general rule, you know—not to make casual acquaintances, I mean."

That sounded dreadfully smug and sedate, she thought. But one *had* to remember the dangers one had known oneself.

"Oh yes—as a general rule." Paula sounded profoundly indifferent to general rules, and Gwyneth's blue eyes were rather troubled as she gazed ahead. She didn't attempt to say anything else until they were seated opposite each other at a veranda table overlooking the river. Then, having ordered tea, she looked across calmly at Paula and said:

"I think you'd better tell me the circumstances of the particular case before you trap me into any more of those dangerous generalities about introductions and no introductions."

Paula was exceedingly taken aback.

"Wh-what particular case?" she asked.

"The one you have in mind."

"I didn't say I had *any* case in mind."

"No, my dear. But one doesn't bother to go so carefully into theoretical cases. I suppose you've met someone very attractive in circumstances which your mother wouldn't think correct."

There was a profound silence.

"That was pretty smart of you," Paula said at last.

"Oh no." Gwyneth gave a rather sad little laugh. "Suppose you tell me."

"Well——" Evidently Paula suddenly made up her mind to talk, and the whole story came tumbling out. "It was when I was in Brussels—at school, you know. At least, not *at* school, of course, but during a week-end I spent with one of the other girls. Her name was Andrée—she was my special friend, and her people had a lovely place in the country. I used to be asked down there quite often. It was one afternoon on the river that we—that we met him. We bumped into his boat. Nothing serious—and, anyway, we were quite near the bank—but we got talking and we offered to let him share our picnic tea——" She paused and looked rather defiantly at Gwyneth.

Gwyneth smiled slightly.

"It doesn't sound a very terrible story yet," she said encouragingly.

"No, of course not. Only it *is* a lot more forthcoming to do that sort of thing in France—Belgium, rather—than it is in England. Andrée was much more doubtful about it than I was."

"Was he Belgian himself?"

"Oh *no*! English."

"Then I presume he was less shocked than Andrée."

Paula laughed.

"*He* wasn't shocked at all."

"No? Well, go on."

"I went down to Andrée's place several week-ends after that and—we met each time."

"Oh. Not by chance every time, surely?"

"No. We arranged it."

"And Andrée was there, too?"

"Yes." There was a slight pause. "Except the last time. I persuaded Andrée to let me go on the river with him alone. She didn't want me to. It wasn't that she was jealous or anything, but, of course, it isn't at all the right thing even now for a well-brought-up foreign girl to go out with a man alone. Andrée thought it was the next thing to being a scarlet woman, I suppose."

"But you persuaded her?"

"Yes, I did." Paula sounded defiant again. "And I'm not sorry."

"No?" Gwyneth remembered that *she* had not been sorry about those many times with Terry—at least, not until afterwards when she found where they had been leading.

"And was that the end of it?" she asked presently.

"No. He was on the same plane when I came back to England."

That time Gwyneth's eyebrows did go up.

"Not by chance again, I take it?"

"No, of course not. I—told him when I was travelling, and he arranged to travel by the same plane. It was—marvellous."

"Then he is in England now?"

"In London."

"I see." Gwyneth frowned. "Are you still seeing him?"

"No." Paula leant forward eagerly. "That's it—that's why I wrote to Van. I didn't know you were going to turn out like this. I thought I'd have to get round Van."

"My dear girl! You didn't seriously suppose that *Van* would assist you to meet someone secretly?"

"Oh no, Gwyneth, not secretly. *Openly.* Don't you see, my parents think Van's frightfully respectable and stern and all that. And your being a Canon's daughter makes it even better——"

Gwyneth experienced a moment's grim amusement at the idea of even her father being pressed into service in the smoothing out of Paula's love affairs.

"I thought," Paula went on, "that if you and Van would bring him along to see my people as a friend of *yours,* it would be quite all right. I can't have him just turn up at the house. Mother would want to know exactly how I met him—and I couldn't tell her flat lies."

"Couldn't you? Oh, I'm glad of that," Gwyneth said

rather dryly. "You mean you want us to tell your lies for you?"

"Oh no!" Paula seemed genuinely taken aback again, and Gwyneth saw that she had considerable difficulty in looking at anything from any point of view but her own. "I didn't mean that exactly."

"Now look here, Paula——" Gwyneth pushed aside her plate and rested her arms on the table. "It's quite true that I would like to be sympathetic and helpful—and, to tell the truth, I don't think Van would be *un*sympathetic about anyone young having a rather better time than your parents might think necessary. But it isn't the slightest good your imagining that we should encourage clandestine meetings and half-truths to your people——"

"But——"

"Just a moment." Gwyneth put her hand firmly on Paula's. "I'm not going to do the heavy relative about the way you met this man. Maybe it wasn't the most discreet way of doing things, but a lot of perfectly good friendships haven't been any more conventionally made. But, without setting up to be faultless myself, I must say you were not very wise about the later steps."

"But, Gwyneth, it just *happened* like that!"

"I thought you said it was arranged."

"Yes. But I mean I couldn't have seen him any other way. They'd have had fifty fits at school if he'd turned up and wanted, quite frankly, to take me out."

"I hope they would. It's the business of schools to be very particular in these matters."

"But don't you see it was a case of never seeing him again if I didn't do it that way—and Andrée *was* there too."

"And it was so necessary to see him again after only one time?"

"Yes," Paula coloured, "it was. I liked him awfully and he felt the same about me."

Gwyneth glanced at the pretty, flushed face opposite. Van had said that was how it had been with him. . . . It was so difficult to tell. . . .

There was a short pause, then Paula said with angry unhappiness:

"We're not getting anywhere, are we?"

"I'm sorry, dear, I was trying to think of a way of helping. You simply won't tell your mother the whole story?"

"I couldn't. She'd say 'How common'—and leave it at that. He'd never be asked near the place."

Gwyneth carefully refrained from commenting on that.

"Well, I'll tell you what I will do," she said slowly. "I'll mention to Van that you've met someone whom you want to bring home, and I'll see if Van will have him along to lunch at his club or something of the sort. I don't want to sound as though your Prince Charming has got to come up for inspection, but I can't take him *only* on your rather prejudiced estimate, you know. If Van thinks well of him, we'll have him and you to dinner together. And after that, I suppose your mother wouldn't mind having him call to see you or take you out."

"Gwyneth," Paula said solemnly, "you're an absolute angel, and, what's more, clever with it."

Gwyneth laughed and got up, pushing back her chair.

"Come along. It's high time we were going. Van will be home and wondering what has happened to us."

"Yes, yes, let's go now." Paula was evidently enchanted at having carried her point in one form or another. "Shall we tell Van this evening?" she asked eagerly as they got back into the car. "How shall we put it?"

"You'll leave that to me," Gwyneth informed her firmly. She had no intention of allowing the whole thing to take on the proportions of a family conspiracy.

"As you like." Paula was apparently willing to trust her future to Gwyneth's judgment, and she made no move to return to the subject during the rapid drive home.

Van was already in and waiting for them.

"Oh, Van, I'm sorry!" Paula immediately took it upon herself to make the excuses. "Have we kept you waiting? I know we've been a long time, but Gwyneth and I have been getting to know each other. She's sweet!"

"I am glad you approve of my choice." Van kissed his wife, and carelessly returned his young cousin's effusive greeting. "I hope she found you bearable."

"Oh yes, we're great friends," Paula asserted. And, declaring she was flattered at the implication, Gwyneth allowed that to stand.

It was a charming, inconsequential sort of evening. Paula
—perhaps because of her successful appeal to Gwyneth—
was in very high spirits, and Van was in one of his rare
and delightful social moods, when he could be both amusing and amused.

"It's the sort of evening when one feels everything must
come right in the end," thought Gwyneth. "Even my little
Toby might somehow come back to me. Not today or tomorrow, perhaps, but some day." And she wondered if
Paula were feeling that everything must come right for
her too.

They finally sent a very happy Paula home by car and
took a taxi themselves.

"She's a nice child," Van remarked with unusual indulgence. "And pretty. It's a pity her parents are quite so
stodgy and old-fashioned about her."

"Yes. I rather think she expects us to fill the roles of indulgent aunt and uncle as an antidote," Gwyneth said with
a smile, to which Van replied rather unexpectedly:

"I don't know that I should mind that."

Gwyneth said nothing more as they drew up outside the
flat, and Van got out and paid the driver. But when the
front door had closed behind them and Van seemed inclined to smoke a last cigarette, she came and sat on the
arm of his chair.

"Paula is very anxious for us to be nice, kind relations
and do something special for her, Van."

"Of course." He regarded the tip of his lighted cigarette
with a dry smile. "I can recall few occasions when young
Paula did *not* want someone to do something special for
her. What is it this time?"

"It seems there's a very romantic young man. She met
him a little unconventionally on a week-end visit to a school
friend who lived just outside Brussels."

"Good lord! A foreigner?" inquired Van disgustedly, in
the best British tradition.

"No, no. An Englishman. She forgot to tell me any
little detail like his name, I've just realized. But, anyway,
it doesn't matter. The point is that she's very much taken
with him and he's turned up now in England—more or less
followed her here, I gather."

"I should think that has agitated the Norbury end of the

axis, hasn't it?" Van unexpectedly put his head against her and, for a moment, Gwyneth forgot Paula's affairs. She put her arm round him and drew him close against her.

"Tired, Van?"

"Not when you do that." He was smiling slightly, and in that moment she was so happy that she wanted everyone else to be happy too—poor little Paula and everyone.

She put her cheek down against his dear, dark hair.

"Are you listening? Shall I go on?"

"What about? Oh, Paula, Yes, if you like."

"She's been seeing this man—or, rather, she did see him quite a lot in Belgium, without her people or the school knowing."

"Disgusting little intriguer," observed Van lazily.

"Oh no, Van! The child hasn't a scrap of real vice in her. Only it mustn't go on like that. There's probably no harm in it, but the principle's all wrong. I've promised we will contrive to push him under her parents' notice in a perfectly creditable way."

"The deuce you have! How are you going to do that? And I wish you could know how adorably absurd you are, endeavouring to be wise and maternal towards an over-confident young woman who is only four or five years younger than you are yourself."

"I'm lots older in most ways."

"Are you, my dear? Well, tell me how you propose to make illicit romance acceptable to Norbury."

"Van, don't call it that."

He moved his head against her so that he could smile up at her.

"Is this a very serious matter?"

"Well, fairly serious. You wouldn't want any harm to come to Paula, would you?"

"Of course not. But, in my opinion, that young woman can look after herself remarkably well. Probably much better than you can, my self-possessed little wife." And, with a quick movement he drew her down on to his knee, so that her head was resting against him this time.

It was so unlike Van to do anything like this, that again she was silent for sheer pleasure. These unexpected tendernesses were so sweet and strange. It was almost as though she discovered all over again how much she loved him, and how hopeless life would be without him.

"Well, what is the next step in the "Save Paula" campaign?"

She laughed reluctantly.

"You must have this man to lunch with you at your club."

"On what pretext?"

"Don't be tiresome, Van. Any pretext, of course. You can make one up—or just say the truth, if you like. You'll have to ring up Paula and find out his name and whereabouts, and what ground you have in common. I don't know what he does for a living."

"Nothing, probably," Van said sceptically. "Young men who can rush back and forth across the Channel in pursuit of a pretty girl usually haven't enough to do."

"Well, maybe he's a free-lance of some sort. Anyway, give him the once-over, will you, Van dear?"

"If you like."

"And then, if he's all right, you might invite him along here to dinner when Paula's coming. After that, she can present him to her parents without having to go into unfortunate details about her first meeting."

Van dropped a kiss on the top of her head.

"For the daughter of a highly-respectable Canon, my dear, you have an astonishing talent for domestic strategy."

"Oh, Van"—she looked troubled—"it sounds stupid and complicated when one goes into all these details—but it was a very harmless little meeting, really. Only unfortunately, her mother's particular brand of conventionality makes difficulties. Paula's a very headstrong girl——"

"She certainly is."

"—And she has rather an idea of herself as one against the world, at the moment. Opposition will merely make her more obstinate and certain that she's being cheated out of a great romance."

"Yes. Silly little idiot," Van observed carelessly.

"Maybe. But *you'd* have been pretty difficult to deal with if you hadn't been allowed to go on seeing me," Gwyneth reminded him with a smile.

"Quite a different matter," Van told her, smiling in his turn. But, after a moment, he added: "All right. I'll look up Paula's Romeo, and follow out the plan of campaign. I hope he's worth all this trouble. And now let's go to bed."

And so they went to bed. And Gwyneth's last thought was:

"How dear and sweet Van is, to have as an ally. If only I could tell him of the real weight on my heart!"

But even that weight was lighter now, because each hour brought her nearer to the day when she was to see her little boy again. It was odd how her mind refused to move any further on than that day. For the moment the future stopped short there.

She didn't know what she hoped from this second visit to the orphanage—certainly nothing concrete. But it seemed that the mere fact of seeing Toby would bring other possibilities to light. She must try to find opportunities to bring Van and the child together. It was no good just telling Van how adorable he was. She must let him see it for himself. And then perhaps——

"Oh, he must love Toby a little," she thought desperately. "He couldn't love me so much and my baby not at all. Besides, Toby feels so sweet, and his voice is so dear and absurd, and his mouth so fresh and damp——"

She had to stop herself from thinking like this, because it made her wild with pain and restlessness. And once she shed a few difficult tears, and Van said something afterwards about her looking as though she had been crying.

You had to be careful—you had to be very careful indeed when your husband knew nothing whatever about your baby, and you were supposed to be a happy and carefree woman.

She played her part well—she knew it. So well, that Van could even tease her unsuspectingly about her favourite, and she could smile carelessly and admit that she was flattered by the little boy's unaccountable partiality.

"It's to be hoped he won't have transferred his allegiance to someone else, or I think your day would be spoilt," Van said with a smile when they were on their way down to Greystones.

"He won't have changed," Gwyneth declared with more quiet confidence than she knew. And only when her husband glanced at her did she realize how odd that must sound.

Once more it was a beautiful day, and Van was driving.

"I suppose there will be some sort of outside display by the children since it's so fine," Van observed.

"Oh, Van, what do they do?"

"The usual things. Some sort of sports competitions or singing. And the very young ones do action songs or a very simple play."

Gwyneth smiled with sheer pleasure. She realized that she was feeling just as any other proud mother might feel —hoping that her darling would be a success and more amusing than any of the others. She didn't know how she would be able to keep from catching him up and hugging him in front of them all.

For the moment, the very anticipation of seeing him was enough. Each minute of the drive was delicious, and she really wanted either to talk of Toby or to be silent.

But Van, unaware of her mood, had other things to say, and presently he remarked with a slight smile:

"I telephoned to Paula about her admirer yesterday, and she gave me his number. Then I rang him up later."

"Oh, did you really?" For a moment she could bear to take her thoughts off Toby. "What did you arrange?"

"That he should lunch with me at the club on Thursday."

"Oh good. I'm so glad. What did he sound like?"

"Very pleasant. Cultured voice. Very pleased to come, I gathered. He's an artist, it seems."

"An artist?" Gwyneth crinkled up the corners of her eyes in a sudden little spasm of nervousness. "What is his name?"

And then she knew, by some horrible instinct, just a second before Van replied:

"Terence Muirkirk. Rather too picturesque. But I suppose he can't very well help his name."

CHAPTER FIVE

FOR a moment Gwyneth thought she must have cried out. The shock was so terrible that she could not imagine she had been able to remain silent. But one terrified glance at Van's unconcerned face told her she had done nothing to betray herself. The world was going on just the same.

Terry had risen from the past, like some fearful ghost. The very foundations of her world were rocking, just as they had that terrible night when she first realized she was going to have Toby. And yet the sun went on shining, the car hummed along the road, Van's hands rested lightly on the wheel, and his expression was calm and unknowing.

"What am I to do?" Gwyneth thought. "What, in God's name, am I to do?—for Paula as well as for myself." Because, of course, she couldn't let Paula go on wandering happily along the edge of a precipice.

Why hadn't she asked Paula the man's name at once? Then she might have put a stop to the whole thing instead of having encouraged it with amiable, well-meaning foolery.

But *how* could she have put a stop to it? Above all, how to put a stop to it now, when she had made things ten times more difficult? Even if she could withdraw their support altogether—by some means make Van refuse to see Terry after all—what then? That only left Paula, in a dangerously miserable and defiant mood, completely at the mercy of Terry—who knew so well how to exploit such a mood.

Suddenly she felt the car slacken speed and stop.

"Gwyneth, you're terribly pale. Aren't you well, child?"

With an effort she opened her eyes and smiled faintly.

"I have a bit of a headache. It's nothing."

Van put his arm round her.

"Would you rather not go? There isn't the slightest need, if you think the heat will make you worse."

"Of course we must go," she cried sharply. And then, because everything seemed to rush at her at once, like a great confusing tide of disaster, she hid her face against Van's shoulder.

She couldn't cope with things. She couldn't possibly disentangle the dreadful skein of events and make them come straight. In sick panic she almost decided to tell Van everything—like a murderer deciding to plead guilty at once, rather than go through the long-drawn-out horror of discovery and trial.

But his quiet: "What is it, my darling?" awakened in her once more the impulse to fight madly for her happiness—her life, almost. These weeks with Van—discovering that,

77

because he loved and trusted her so much, he could be far more tender and demonstrative than she had ever supposed—they couldn't be sacrificed lightly. If only she could escape from this danger all her life could be like these last weeks with Van. She must go on. So long as there was the smallest, weakest chance of rescuing such happiness, she must go on.

Raising her head, she smiled with creditable composure into Van's anxious eyes.

"It's all right, really. Only when you put your arm round me I always want to cling to you and forget everything else."

"Oh, Gwyn dear!" His laugh was both relieved and moved. "And you're sure there is nothing wrong?—that you will be perfectly well?"

"Quite sure."

He looked at her consideringly for a moment longer, but he seemed satisfied with the scrutiny.

"Very well. Take it quietly for the rest of the way and perhaps the headache will wear off."

"I'm sure it will."

She watched him start up the car again—idly watched the needle of the speedometer rising, the hedges slipping past on either side. A sort of numbness had come over her, and the raging fever of agitation had dropped. By and by she would realize again how helplessly she was trapped, but for the moment she could take in no more. She could only yield thankfully to the temporary drug of Van's tenderness, which would never change—until he knew.

The sharp stab of that thought shocked the colour from her face again, and then she made another effort to quieten her mind, because Van must be kept from suspecting anything.

As the car turned into the long drive leading to Greystones, she thought:

"Perhaps I can make Paula see reason. Perhaps, if I tell her a little of what happened"—she winced at the thought—"I can persuade her to give up thinking about him." And then: "No, I couldn't tell her anything near the real truth, of course. I should have to pretend it happened to a friend of mine—and then not all the details. But oh,

God! that weakens the whole case so terribly. Paula wouldn't even listen. She's so sure she knows best——"

"We're here, Gwyn," Van said, and she turned to smile at him quite tranquilly—just as though her thoughts were not rushing to and fro like frightened, trapped little animals.

Greystones was looking very delightful in the sunshine, and several very handsome cars were already lined up outside. As they went into the big entrance hall Gwyneth had the impression of quite an important social gathering.

"It's a beautiful place, isn't it?" people said to each other a dozen times over. And one woman added: "One feels it is all so *worthwhile* when one sees the children with almost every advantage they would have in a good home of their own."

"Yes. Oh, quite," murmured several voices dutifully. And one of the younger women said gaily:

"Who *wouldn't* be an orphan in circumstances like these?"

There was a little ripple of laughter, and Gwyneth even managed to laugh, too, while she thought:

"My darling, my darling, where are you? When will all these stupid preliminaries be over, so that I can see you and hold you and talk to you? They don't understand, these people. How could they? If they have children themselves, they're safe and happy in their own homes. They don't know what it's like just to see their children for one day and then go away again."

To all these people she was simply Evander Onslie's charming young wife—just married, you know—not a care in the world. They couldn't possibly have visualized her as a wretched, guilty, troubled woman, hoping against hope that she would be able to snatch a few moments alone with her baby.

"Have you seen the new dormitory?" "Yes, charming, isn't it?" "The gardens are looking so attractive." "Lucky children—so much space." "Oh, but you must see the kitchens—quite models, you know." "I hear we can go and see the tinies have their lunch, if we like. They do everything for themselves, I understand."

"Van!" She caught her husband's arm. "Someone says we can go and see the very little ones have lunch. Let's go.

The visitors aren't having lunch until much later. There's plenty of time."

Van smiled and came with her to the square, light dining-room where about two dozen children, between the ages of four and seven, were seated at half a dozen tables, very much interested in the food before them, very little interested in the one or two visitors who looked in on them.

Gwyneth saw him at once—on duty, apparently—very important—carrying round a dish of carrots from which each child helped himself.

"There's your little friend," murmured Van, and she nodded—partly because she was too much absorbed to speak, partly because there was a lump in her throat.

The distribution of carrots was almost complete by now. And then suddenly Toby looked up from his task and saw her.

She had not known it was possible for his dear little face to look so beautiful. His eyes went very big and dark, and he stood quite still, smiling at her until she thought her heart would burst.

"Toby!" hissed four sibilant whispers from four hungry companions, still awaiting their turn.

He pushed the dish, unceremoniously under their astonished little noses, and, breaking away from the group of tables, he ran to Gwyneth, where she stood by the door.

Almost choking with a fearful sort of joy, she caught him up in her arms. No doubt it was against the rules. No doubt Van was thinking it all very extraordinary. She couldn't help it. He was her baby. His arms were round her neck and his mouth on hers. She thought she would die of sheer happiness.

"How d'you do. I must go now," he said, beginning to scramble down. She wanted to hold him, but he said again: "I must go now," as though nations waited on his actions.

So she had to let him go then, but he kept on glancing round over his shoulder and smiling at her, as though he hoped she were watching his every movement.

"Oh, Van, isn't he sweet?" she whispered to her husband.

"He's adorable," Van said slowly. And then she wanted to cling to him and sob:

"Oh, please, please can I take him home and keep him?" But instead she had to behave with perfect self-control.

She could have watched Toby for hours, but presently the request was brought that they would come and have lunch themselves. And Gwyneth had to tear herself away, and go and make pleasant conversation to strangers in the now transformed staff dining-room.

"Did you see the little ones having lunch all on their own? Weren't they cute?" someone said to Gwyneth, and she saw it was the young, gay woman who had exclaimed: "Who wouldn't be an orphan here?"

"Yes," Gwyneth said, "I saw them."

"There was one killing little pet taking round vegetables. I could have picked him up and run away with him," her companion declared. And Gwyneth wanted to say angrily:

"Oh no, you couldn't! He's mine."

As it was, her husband answered for her:

"That was Toby, I expect. My wife and he are quite old friends."

"I do love Van!" Gwyneth thought with passionate gratitude. "How dear of him to make Toby sound almost mine!"

"Oh, you *know* him? Dear me, you are honoured. He wouldn't take the slightest notice of any of us. He was much too busy."

"Yes, he takes things very seriously," Gwyneth said tenderly, and she felt her husband glance at her again.

"I hear there's an entertainment by the children afterwards—on the lawn. That ought to be fun. I hope little sobersides is in it."

"I hope so," Gwyneth smiled rather coldly, because this stupid woman didn't seem to realize that darling Toby could be very laughing and jolly, too. He was only serious when there were serious matters on hand.

And then again she thought: "I'm just like any other mother—anxious that everyone should think her darling perfect."

After lunch, she and Van strolled out on to the lawn to see the improvised stage which had been put up there. It looked very festive, with bunting and coloured butter muslin, and the dark trees behind made a beautiful background.

People strolled about, smoking and talking, and every now and then an eager little figure or two would pop out from behind the high stage to inspect the scene. But an unseen authority always called them back again.

There were deck chairs scattered about, and Gwyneth and Van sat down quite near the stage.

"How is the headache, Gwyn?"

"Oh, quite gone." She turned an almost radiant face on him. Not all the grim problems closing in on her could spoil the exquisite enjoyment of this afternoon near Toby.

Preparations were complete at last, and the great business of the entertainment began—with some very creditable chorus singing from the older children. They had fresh, young voices which sounded very sweet in the open air, and at any other time, Gwyneth would have been charmed. But now she was like some admirer waiting for a stage star—she could not take much interest in anything until he should come on to the scene.

He made his appearance at last, in a little action play for the younger ones. First she recognized the decorative Freddie in the character of Cupid—so glamorous in his scanty attire and clutching his bow and arrows that he raised a round of applause on his own. This rather went to his head and, forsaking his pensive pose at the back of the stage, he came forward and beamed at his admiring public.

It was only with great difficulty that he was persuaded to come off the stage at all, after that—to make way for two indignant little heralds who had been dancing with impatience to make their entry for the last three minutes.

They blew upon two tin trumpets with great gusto and slowly a diminutive magician came into view. He was in black, with silver stars pasted on his long robe, and from under the high, conical hat looked out the solemn features of Toby.

With great dignity and self-possession he paced up and down the platform, entirely oblivious of the ripples of delighted laughter, and slowly waved his wand to and fro.

It was at that exact moment that disaster broke on the pleasant, amusing scene. Almost as though the child's action had really raised some force of evil, a rapid tongue of fire seemed to run like lightning up the bunting at the side of the stage, and the muslin which draped the platform suddenly became one swirl of flame.

"Toby!"

She was on her feet and racing across the intervening space almost before anyone else realized what was happening. The two heralds had scuttled for safety, but Toby stood where he was, fascinated with horror at the smoke and flames all round him.

"Toby! Jump, darling—I'll catch you."

She was almost against the stage, but it was too high for her to reach him, and the flames leapt out at her as though they meant to drive her back.

She scarcely even noticed them as she repeated her cry to the scared little figure in the absurd magician's robes.

For a moment he didn't seem even to hear her voice—then suddenly he saw her, and with a little yelp of relief, he rushed towards her.

He was frightened of the jump and frightened of the flames, but she held up her arms to him and smiled.

As he jumped, her thin frock burst into flame.

With a gasp of horror, she flung the child clear and tore at the blazing dress. Someone seized her—Van, she knew, from the strength of the hands which tried to crush out the flames—but the thin dress blazed like a torch.

A coat was flung round her, and then another. Scarcely knowing what she was doing, she struggled frantically.

"Don't, darling—you're all right. I have you," she heard Van say. And then she fainted.

Afterwards they told her that the whole thing, from start to finish, took only two or three minutes, but it had seemed to her like hours. And the blank unconsciousness which succeeded it seemed to have continued for days, when at last she struggled to the surface again.

She was lying in a room she didn't know at all, but she knew the tall figure standing at the window, with his back to her.

"Van," she said rather weakly, and he turned at once and came over to her, his face so pale and strained that he looked much older than she had ever seen him look before.

She smiled—more faintly than she knew—and whispered:

"I'm all right. Where is Toby?"

Van put his hand very lightly on her hair.

"The baby's all right, too. You have nothing to worry about."

She thought how delightful it was to have Van speak of Toby like that.

"Can I see him?"

"Not just now, dear. It's quite late at night. He's in bed."

She saw then that the light was on, and that Van had really been gazing out into the darkness. There were a lot of things she wanted to ask, but they were all too much trouble. So she just smiled at him again and closed her eyes instead.

When she opened them once more it was morning, and everything was much clearer and sharper in her mind. She guessed that the little white room where she was lying was part of the orphanage, and she supposed from the throbbing in her left arm and shoulder that this was where she had suffered most from burns yesterday.

Van was not there any longer, and she wondered unhappily if he had gone back to London. Business was so very much part of Van's life. Then she remembered that it was Sunday, and there would be nothing to take him away from her. Even as she thought that, the door opened and he came into the room.

"Hello, Van." She saw a profoundly relieved expression come over his face as she greeted him. "I was afraid for a moment that you'd gone back to London."

"Gone back to London? You couldn't have thought that." He bent down and kissed first her cheek and then her lips.

"Well, I'd forgotten it was Sunday and that you didn't have to go to the office."

"You don't really think the office or anything else would have taken me away from you just now, do you?"

"N-no, I suppose not." She considered that and then asked curiously: "I'm not *very* ill, am I?"

He didn't answer directly.

"You had a very nasty shock," was what he said. "That was more serious than the burns."

"I think *you* had a bad shock too, Van." She put up her uninjured hand to touch his cheek.

"Yes," he said briefly, and she saw him press his lips together hard.

"You mustn't worry any more now," she told him and, pulling him down feebly, she kissed him.

He sat down on the side of the bed, then, and presently she said: "Put your arm round me, Van."

He did so at once, drawing her into the circle of his arm, so that she could lean against him.

"All right like that?"

"Um-hm."

They were both silent, and then, after a minute or two, they both became aware of a certain amount of scrambling and panting outside the door of the room. The handle turned jerkily at last, the door opened slowly, and into the room came Toby.

On seeing Van he looked so taken aback that it was pretty obvious he was not really supposed to be paying this unofficial call.

"Did you want me, darling?" Gwyneth asked gently, and he transferred his solemn gaze to her.

"Yes, I want you," he said, but he didn't move.

It was Van who held out his hand.

"Come along, then."

Toby trotted across the room then and stood by the bed staring at her afresh.

"Van, he can't reach me there."

Van lifted the child on to the bed beside her.

"Careful, now."

But the warning was not really necessary. Toby was very careful not to touch her bandaged arm as he put his arms round her neck and hugged her.

Van looked down at them both with a very odd expression. He still had one arm round Gwyneth, so that, in a way, he was holding them both now.

"Are you all right, Toby?" She patted his cheek and looked at him with anxious, loving eyes.

"Yes, thank you, I'm all right," Toby said in his gruff little voice. "Are you all right?"

She nodded with a smile. And Toby looked up then at Van and repeated benevolently: "Are you all right, too?"

"Oh yes, thank you."

"Don't your hands hurt any more?"

"Van!" Gwyneth caught hold of one of his hands in a startled way. "Were your hands hurt?"

"It was nothing. Only a little scorching. See, it's almost all right, even now."

"Oh, my dear, that was when you caught hold of me and tried to put the flames out?"

"Yes."

She turned over the hand she was holding and lightly kissed the palm. Toby watched with great interest.

"Why do you do that?" he wanted to know.

"To make it all right again," Van said.

"Because I love him," Gwyneth said at the same moment, and she felt Van's arm tighten almost convulsively.

Toby examined the hand in his turn.

"And did that make it all right again?"

"Perfectly, thank you," Van assured him gravely.

"I'm glad," Toby said kindly, and lying back on the bed he began to sing, with an air of elaborate unconcern.

When he sang, the deep pitch of his voice was even funnier than when he spoke, and both Gwyneth and Van smiled irresistibly.

"That's a very nice song, Toby," Gwyneth observed when he had finished.

"Yes," Toby sat up again and with great eagerness. "It's my 'gician's song. There wasn't time to sing it yesterday," he added in a slightly aggrieved tone, and Gwyneth saw, to her relief, that the child had no very deep impression of his terrible experience. His chief regret was that he not been able to sing his carefully prepared song.

"I'm so sorry about that," Gwyneth told him.

"Shall I sing it again now?" Toby offered, with thinly veiled determination, and Van said: "If you must," while she said: "Yes, please do."

So he sang it again, to his own complete satisfaction.

Just at that moment there was a knock at the door and the matron looked in.

"Mrs. Onslie, have you seen——Oh, there he is. Toby, you must come along with me now. And you mustn't bother Mrs. Onslie like this, you know. You must ask first if you may come."

"He doesn't bother me," Gwyneth said with a faint smile. "Can't he stay a little longer?"

But it was Van who said:

"I think the matron is right, Gwyneth." And reluctantly she realized that perhaps she was too tired to want to talk any more.

When Toby had gone she and Van were silent again.

She glanced up at him, and again was struck by the stern pallor of his face and the slight lines round his eyes which made him look very much his age. Poor Van! He must have thought for those dreadful minutes yesterday that he had lost her. As she had said, he looked now like a man who had received a very bad shock.

He was not looking at her just then. He was gazing away out of the window, and the way his dark eyes narrowed and his nostrils distended slightly gave the impression that he was living over again a very unpleasant experience.

"Van dear——" She pressed against him in that way he loved, and his eyes came back to her face, unsmiling at first, even when they lighted on her. "You mustn't worry any more. You have me here safe in your arms. Nothing else matters."

She was half startled at the effect that had. He bit his lips so hard that there was a thin line of scarlet where his teeth had clamped down on it. And he held her close and said in a queerly roughened voice: "I know, I know. You're quite right. Nothing else really matters. Nothing, nothing, nothing!"

During the next few days Gwyneth began to regain her strength again. The doctor repeated what Van had said— that the shock had been more serious than the burns, and she was kept very quiet. For a great part of the time Van was with her, and there were fairly frequent visits from Toby, which made her very happy.

After the first two days Van went up to town for a few hours each day, but he would not leave her altogether, and every evening he came back again to her—though, as Mrs. Kellaby said with a smile: "Not many husbands would come all the way down to Hampshire each evening, just to say good night."

It was Mrs. Kellaby who gave Gwyneth some details of what had happened on the day of the disastrous entertainment.

"We can only think that someone must have been careless with cigarette ash when they were strolling about beforehand," she said. "A lot of people did go to examine the stage and the decorations, you know."

"Yes, I remember. We did ourselves."

"No doubt. It must have been that a spark dropped on some of the muslin which was trailing on the grass. It would smoulder slowly most likely because, if you remember, there had been some rain overnight and the grass was damp. Then, of course, as soon as the fire reached the dry part of the muslin, the whole thing blazed up."

"Yes." Gwyneth shivered. "It all seemed to happen so terribly quickly."

what was the matter. I can't tell you how much we are indebted to you ourselves, Mrs. Onslie, apart from any other consideration."

"It did happen quickly. You realized, before anyone else,

"Oh, that's all right," Gwyneth smiled faintly. It was rather funny, being thanked for having saved her own little boy.

"You are quite a heroine among the younger children, I can assure you. And as for Toby, of course—he really talks of very little else."

"He's such a dear little boy," Gwyneth said softly. "I—I could quite wish he belonged to me. I suppose it wouldn't be possible for—for me to have him home for a while— a sort of holiday for him?"

"It's odd you should ask that." Mrs. Kellaby looked thoughtful. "Your husband had the same idea."

"*Did* he?"

"Yes. I suppose it was because he saw how taken you were with Toby, and he thought, while you were ill, it might be nice to think of something you would like very much. He spoke to my husband about it."

Oh, dear, dear Van! How good and unselfish he was, for all his autocratic ways. He wanted her to have something that would give her great pleasure, because he was so sorry and worried that she was ill.

"What—did Dr. Kellaby think about it? In her eagerness Gwyneth could not quite keep her voice from trembling.

"Well, of coure, you know, it would be quite outside any of our rules. To be quite candid, we don't think it's at all a good idea to let the children see much of ordinary private home life. It is calculated to make them fret rather when they have to come back to institutional life."

"Yes, I—do see—that." She thought of Toby, fretting

because he had been in the home which should be his and then had to come back here. It made her throat ache.

"Of course," Mrs. Kellaby went on reflectively, "there *have* been cases of adoption from Greystones——"

"Yes?"

"Naturally you wouldn't want to do anything in a hurry, but perhaps it is in your mind that the visit might develop into something permanent?"

"Mrs. Kellaby"—Gwyneth sat up eagerly—"I'll be quite frank with you. That is the idea at the back of *my* mind. But of course, my husband hasn't got as far as that yet. He—well, he's less impulsive than I am, and I suppose a man doesn't get so carried away by an idea. Only I did hope that if Toby were with us in our own home, it wouldn't take Van long to get so fond of him that *he* wouldn't want the child to go back either. That's—that's why it's so important that we should be allowed to have him for a visit."

"I see. I thought perhaps there was something like that behind it."

Gwyneth gazed at the Superintendent's wife with painful eagerness.

"Do you think Dr. Kellaby would consider it? I mean, if my husband does really entertain the idea."

"He probably would in those circumstances."

"But of course, it wouldn't do to suggest ultimate adoption just yet."

"No, I see that. Shall I speak to him about it?"

"Oh, I wish you would." Gwyneth clasped Mrs. Kellaby's hand with nervous gratitude. "So that when—*if* Van does ask him some more about it, he will be in a favourable mood."

Mrs. Kellaby smiled rather at this idea of practising strategy on her husband. Then her expression changed again and she looked at Gwyneth with kindly seriousness.

"There is one other thing, you know, my dear. You're very young and very near the beginning of your marriage to think of adopting a child. An adopted child can be quite a serious problem if you have children of your own later."

"I should love Toby just as though—just as though he were my own," Gwyneth protested quickly.

"No, it isn't quite the same thing. Much better realize

that from the beginning. And your husband certainly wouldn't feel it was the same thing."

Gwyneth was silent. She didn't want to hear the reasons against Toby's coming to her. She wanted reassuring, if anything. She wanted to be told that it was a wonderful, safe, splendid idea.

Perhaps her wistful expression touched Mrs. Kellaby. At any rate, she patted Gwyneth's hand and said:

"Don't think I am trying to dissuade you, but anything as serious as the possibility of adopting a child must be looked at from every angle. Anyway, talk it over with your husband and see how he feels about it."

"I will," Gwyneth said, and she managed to smile quite calmly in reply.

When Van came in that evening it was already getting late. He had been delayed in town and had had dinner on the way down, when he found he could not arrive at a reasonable hour.

"Oh, Van dear, it's really much too tiring for you to do this double journey every day." She hugged him with some of her old energy as she returned his kiss. But he shook his head and said:

"It's worth it when I get here. Had a good day, darling?"

"Yes, lovely. I'm lots stronger now and I can soon be moved back home."

"That will be good."

"Yes, I shall be thankful too. Though they're very, very kind here. And—and I shall miss having Toby coming in and out to see me."

Van didn't say anything for a moment and she saw that rather strained look return. It tugged at her heartstrings and made her feel wretchedly remorseful. Was he really trying to screw himself to do something he disliked intensely because he knew it would give her pleasure? Oh, she didn't want him to have to do that! And yet how else was she to have Toby?

"He'll grow to love him," Gwyneth told herself agitatedly. "He'd *have* to. He couldn't help it. It's only a question of getting used to the idea at first."

She looked up at him.

"What is it, Van?" Her heart beat quickly, but she managed to smile carelessly.

He sat down slowly on the side of the bed, in his favourite position with his arm round her.

"You're terribly anxious to have Toby home, really, aren't you?"

"Well, I——" And then, to her horror, she suddenly began to cry, so desperately and wildly that she thought he must surely know exactly what was the matter.

"Don't, child! Don't, don't cry like that." He held her close and kissed her hair and her neck, because she would not look up and let him kiss her face. "I didn't know you wanted him so badly. You shall have him. You shall have whatever you want, but for God's sake, don't distress yourself like this."

"Oh, I'm so sorry——It's so absurd—I didn't mean—"

"Hush, darling." His voice was exceedingly tender. "You don't have to explain. You're nervous and upset still. And saving the child from danger made him even dearer to you."

"Yes, yes—that's it. I've been wondering and wondering how I could make you understand—make you want him, too. I thought and thought, and all the time I got more nervous, and then when there wasn't any need after all, I—oh, it's so stupid!"

"It's not stupid, my dear. It's perfectly natural." (Oh, if he knew how natural!) "Only there wasn't any real need to be nervous. I'm very sorry now that I ever refused you at first."

"No, that was natural, too," she whispered as she put her arms up round his neck and hugged him with almost childlike fervour. "It was odd to—to want to have Toby to stay with us from the first moment I saw him. It must have seemed unkind and unreasonable to you. It's difficult to account for these impulses." She glanced at him nervously, but he was accepting what she had said quite calmly. "It wasn't *only* a simple impulse, Van."

"I know, dear. He is a very lovable child, and he seems to have the same instinctive affection for you that you have for him. As you say, one can't always account for these things."

"N-no, one can't."

Oh, blessed, blessed relief that it seemed a fairly natural

thing to Van! He even sounded already as though he might not necessarily consider the visit a purely temporary affair. She glanced at him timidly again.

"Van, you do like him, too, don't you?"

"Of course, child. No one could help it."

"And you won't mind having him for this visit?"

"No, certainly not. Particularly if it's going to make you so happy."

Her smile assured him of that.

"Shall I speak to Kellaby about it?"

"Oh, Van, I wish you would."

"Then I'll go and have a word with him now. I had mentioned the possibility already."

"And he didn't absolutely refuse?"

"Oh no." Van's smile was slightly grim. "He didn't absolutely refuse." And Gwyneth thought that perhaps there were not many people with sufficient courage to refuse Van anything absolutely.

She watched him go out of the room, and then lay there alone in the soft lamp-light, a great quiet stealing over her, so that she felt tranquil in a way she had not known since childhood.

In spite of everything—the anxiety, the fear, the nerve-strain—she dozed contentedly, and when he came back to her much later, she was already drifting in the borderland between sleeping and waking.

Something in her sleepy content must have amused as well as touched him, because she heard him laugh softly.

"All right, darling. Go to sleep now." He bent down and kissed her—but too lightly to wake her entirely. "We can have Toby for a month. I'll take you both back home as soon as the doctor will let you travel."

"Oh, Van, I do love you," she whispered, and fell asleep, still smiling.

The next morning it seemed there was no need for Van to go to London early. He came in and had breakfast with her, and he was still there when Toby came to pay his usual morning call.

Gwyneth was up and in an armchair that morning, and the change interested Toby immensely.

"Are you better?" He came and planted his small hands on the blanket which covered her knees.

"Oh yes, thank you, Toby. Lots better."

"Can you walk again?"

"I expect so."

"Let me see."

"No, no, not just now." Van spoke for the first time and rather sternly.

Toby leant against Gwyneth's chair and said in a loud whisper:

"Do you have to do what that man tells you?"

Gwyneth laughed.

"No, I don't have to. But I like to. He's my husband, you know."

"Oh."

She glanced at Van and said in an undertone: "Do you suppose he knows yet?"

"I shouldn't think so."

"Shall I tell him?"

"I see no harm in it."

"Tell what?" Toby looked interestedly from one to the other. "Tell me, tell me!" And he began to get on to Gwyneth's knee.

She hugged the little figure up against her and laughed.

"Did anyone tell you that you were going to have a holiday?"

He shook his head.

"And be a 'gician and sing my song?" he asked eagerly.

"No, not that sort of holiday. Not just a day, but a whole month—with me. Would you like to come and live with me for a month?"

"Yes, please."

He couldn't quite take it in, she saw.

"And Freddie and Kevin and Gordon, too?" he wanted to know.

"No, just you."

He began to smile slowly.

"Can I take Toby Two?"

"Oh yes. You can take anything you like."

"And live with you?"

"Yes. And with my husband, too."

"In a little house?"

"Well, in a flat."

"Why is it flat? I never saw a flat house."

"No. It's part of a very big house."

"Like this one?"

"Oh no—I can't explain." She laughed and hugged him, and then he laughed, too, because she did. "We'll take you in a big motor-car all the way to London. And I'll take you to see the parks and the shops and we'll go to the Zoo and see all the animals, and you shall choose what we shall have for tea every day, and have a little room all to yourself—and we'll be perfectly happy——"

As she spoke his cheeks grew pinker and pinker and his eyes rounder and rounder.

"Chocolate biscuits!" he cried as she paused.

"Do you want chocolate biscuits?"

"Yes, please. For tea. That's what I'll choose."

"What?—every day?"

"Yes, please. Every day."

She laughed again. It was so easy to laugh when Toby was there. "Are you happy, Toby?" She kissed his pink cheek.

"Yes, thank you, I'm happy." He kissed her in return. And then suddenly his eye fell on Van who was standing watching this scene with a slight smile.

"Did he say I could come, too?" Toby indicated Van with an unmistakable finger.

"Oh yes, of course."

Toby and Van looked at each other, both with a faintly doubtful expression. Then the little boy slid slowly off Gwyneth's knee and went over to him.

"What?" Van looked down from his great height.

Toby held up his face.

For a moment Van didn't realize what he wanted. When he did, Gwyneth saw him flush quite darkly. A little awkwardly he picked up the child and looked at him.

Toby's doubts were already gone. He beamed at Van like a benevolent elf.

"What do you want?"

For the first time since she had known him, Gwyneth detected the faintest touch of nervousness in Van's tone.

"To kiss you," Toby said unblushingly.

A very odd expression came into Van's dark eyes. And then he and Toby solemnly exchanged a kiss.

CHAPTER SIX

"CAN I push that thing that does the "honk-honk" again?"

"No, not just now."

"Does that clock tick?"

"Yes, I expect so."

"Can I listen to it?"

"If you like, but you won't hear much above the sound of the car."

"Have we gone a thousand miles yet?"

"No, not quite."

They were on their way home to London at last, and Toby, sitting in the front seat between Van and Gwyneth, was putting Van through a catechism to which he was submitting remarkably well. Almost everything they passed was new to the little boy and he was wild with pleasure and curiosity.

"Is this London?" he asked almost every time they came to the outskirts of a village, and Gwyneth had to assure him that London was still a long way further on.

By the time they did reach the outer suburbs he was actually fast asleep, worn out with excitement and the pleasures of discovery.

Van glanced at him and laughed.

"Has it all been a bit too much for him?"

"Just a little, I think. Oh, Van, how nice it is to be back."

"Yes. It's pretty good, isn't it?"

When they finally reached the flat, she tried to wake Toby up. But Van said:

"Here, let me take him. He's too heavy for you." And, picking the child up, he carried him into the building.

Betty, the maid who opened the door to them, smiled at Gwyneth and asked her how she was, with great solicitude.

"Quite a heroine you were, madam," she observed with admiration. "And this is the little boy?"

"Yes, this is the little boy," Van said, and handed him over to Betty.

Toby was beginning to rub his eyes now.

"I want to go to London," he said firmly, if sleepily, and was very pleased when Betty assured him he was already there.

"Is this a flat house?" He looked round admiringly.

"A flat," Gwyneth amended, but without much expectation of changing his own description of it.

"I'll take him and give him his bath, madam, and then, perhaps, you would like him to have his supper in the lounge."

"Please, Betty."

When Betty and the little boy had departed, she wandered round the room saying: "Oh, Van, how lovely everything is! I'd forgotten how lovely."

He looked up with a slight laugh from his writing-desk.

"It's only lovely when you're here," he told her.

"Thanks, darling. I return the compliment."

She leant on the back of his chair and smiled down at him. She felt so light-hearted, for were not Van and Toby both hers for a whole month?

He was very much aware of her, she knew, because of the faint smile which just touched her mouth, but he appeared to be almost completely absorbed in the papers on his desk.

"Oh, that's for you." He handed over his shoulder a sheet torn from a memorandum pad. "It's the address and phone number of Paula's Terry What's-his-name."

She took the paper and straightened up slowly.

"You'll need it." He went on writing as he talked. "I told him you'd be writing to invite him here as soon as we were back and you felt well enough."

"Of course—you saw him, didn't you? Had lunch with him while I was down at Greystones?" She slowly curled the piece of paper in her fingers.

"I did."

"What did you think of him?" She was glad she was standing behind him.

"Oh, pleasant enough fellow. I suppose a woman would call him good-looking. He's travelled a lot—talks quite interestingly. Considering Paula picked him up abroad, she might have done much worse."

"Might she?"

"Definitely." Van had only half his attention on the matter now.

She went and sat down in a low chair, near the fire which had been lighted as the evening had turned cool.

There was a hysterical desire in her to say: "He's Toby's

father, you know," and see how that would shatter the calm atmosphere of the room and her husband's preoccupation. But she was silent—staring into the fire, pretending to warm her hands.

It was not that she had forgotten the sword hanging over her—and, still more, over Paula. Only, in the excitement and happiness of having Toby, everything else had become remote and unreal. The difficulties there had seemed to roll away magically at a touch from Van. It had seemed as though all other difficulties must surely do the same.

But now she was home again, and grim realities were gathering round. In her hands was a paper bearing Terry's name and address. She had to write to him—invite him into her home—speak with him—perhaps match her wits against his. And in all this she would not have Van's help this time. She had to do it alone.

The door opened just then and Toby came in, dressed in pyjamas and a dressing-gown, the cord of which trailed behind him in majestic abandon.

"I've had my bath," he announced. "And there was green soap. But Betty says green soap doesn't taste any nicer than white soap. Doesn't green soap taste nice?"

"No, dear," Gwyneth secured the dressing-gown cord and tied it round him, while he smiled at her all the time.

"I like London," he said. "And I like flat houses and green soap. And I like Betty," he added graciously, as Betty came in with a bowl of bread and milk, and two chocolate biscuits on a little plate.

They put him in a low chair and let him have a small table all to himself, which delighted him hugely.

"Look at me!" he cried invitingly to Van.

"Why?" But Van looked up and smiled across at him.

"Because I have a table all to myself."

"Very exclusive."

"What's sclusive?" he asked Gwyneth, and while she tried to explain, he spooned up his bread and milk, and occasionally paused to rearrange his two chocolate biscuits on their plate.

It was a wonderful first evening.

For Gwyneth it was a wonderful first evening, too. But in the background, there was always the shadow of Terry.

During the next few days she tried to put off her decision. It was not necessary to have him here at once. She might surely let herself enjoy Toby for a very short while first—the morning walks, the meals together, the little expeditions.

But while she was doing this, in what sort of danger was Paula? Paula—who, if she grew impatient, would certainly yield to any pleading of Terry's that she would meet him secretly.

"I'll have to see Paula and tell her the truth," Gwyneth told herself desperately. But the very next moment she thought: "No, I can't, I can't! I hardly know her. She is anything but discreet. I *can't* put my whole happiness in her hands".

Then—what?

And slowly, out of her sheer despair another idea began to grow. There was just one other chance—one faint possibility of settling the whole business without having to tell Paula anything.

She could force Terry to see her.

The decision was so simple and yet so momentous that it frightened her even to think that she was anywhere near carrying it out. On the terrible day long ago, when he had left her in that third-rate hotel, she had never thought to see him again. Even now she had hardly brought herself to believe that she would have to meet him, even in company with other people, and with the protecting knowledge that he could not say anything to her outside the barest conventionalities.

That she should see him alone—speak to him of intimate things—appeal to his better feelings, which she knew were almost non-existent—or, perhaps, even try to threaten him —all these seemed fantastic. But they were also beginning to seem horribly inevitable too.

How else was she to hold back the terrible march of events? How rescue Paula—and probably herself, too— from absolute disaster?

A whole night of wretched self-questioning and attempts to find other ways to escape finally hardened her resolve.

The next morning, when Van had gone to the office, she sat down to write to Terry. And, once she had started the letter, the words flowed with extraordinary ease.

You may not be altogether surprised to receive this letter (she wrote), because I don't know if anything which Paula or Van may have said has identified me for you. But—in case you don't know—I married Van Onslie some months ago and, by some irony of fate, it was me whom Paula first told about her friendship with you. Even then, she didn't mention your name, and it was not until later that I realized the position.

You and I shall probably have to meet in the future—indeed, I think Van has already invited you home. But before that happens I must speak with you alone. Will you please telephone to me some time tomorrow, between eleven and five, so that we can arrange it?—
                                        Gwyneth.

She addressed the letter, and, with a sort of sick determination, dropped it into the nearest pillar-box.

Several times during the evening she wondered if Van noticed anything strange in her manner. Toby had said twice that afternoon:

"Have you got a headache? Do you feel quiet?" And each time she had assured him that she was all right, and had told herself that she must manage better than this.

But Van only said:

"You're rather tired, child, aren't you? Have you been overdoing it to-day?"

"No, Van. But I am a little tired. I think I'll go to bed early."

So she had to go to bed early—which brought the dreaded tomorrow all the more quickly.

She hated every minute of the next morning. Each time the telephone bell rang, her heart seemed to flutter in her throat. And each time it was something quite unimportant, something which surely, surely need not have been used to drag at her nerves on this morning of all mornings.

And then, when the terrible moment did at last arrive, it was Toby who, on a sudden naughtly impulse, seized up the telephone and cried "Hello", as he had seen her do.

She took the receiver from him at once, and told him to run along to Betty. And, even as she spoke, she heard Terry's well-known voice say:

"Mrs. Onslie? Gwyneth, is that you?"

"Yes——" She got it out somehow. "Yes. Is that Terry?"

"Of course. It was charming to hear from you."

She wondered then how that faintly insolent voice could ever have held such charm for her. But of course, the tone had been very different then—just as the tone which he used to Paula now would be different.

"Terry, where can I meet you?" She couldn't bring herself to say any tactful things to lead up to the question. She must get it over as quickly as possible.

"Are you quite sure you want to see me?"

"No, but I must. It's necessary."

He laughed slightly then.

"We-ell——"

"Where can I see you?" She spoke impatiently because she hated having to repeat the question, as though it were of such importance to see him. Her pride had never been very much in evidence when she had had dealings with him before. Now the position was very different, and her pride suffered badly.

"You'd better come along here, to my rooms," he said carelessly.

"To your—rooms? I don't think that's necessary."

"But very enjoyable, don't you think? And safer than meeting in a public place."

"I'll take that risk," she said curtly. "I don't want to come to your rooms."

"My dear Gwyneth, you surely aren't troubling about the conventions at this hour, are you? I should have thought we had shared a room too often for that to matter."

She hated him so much when he said that that for a moment she could not even reply. When she did, it was simply to repeat:

"I prefer not to come to your rooms."

"And I prefer that you should, my dear," he said dryly. "It happens to suit me better. If you want to see me—you'll find me here any time during this afternoon. If you don't come, I shall know that you decided it was better for us *not* to meet."

She began to say something else—to protest again, but the line went dead, and she was left sitting there with the telephone receiver in her hand, while the certainty was growing on her that it was almost useless to go and see him in any case.

Yet she had to go. What else could she do? It was the only possible chance.

At lunch-time Toby said to her:

"Am I coming out with you this afternoon?"

"Not this afternoon, darling. I have to go out alone. Betty will take you out."

"Oh." He looked rather dashed. He was great friends with Betty, but nothing was quite so much fun as going out with Gwyneth. "Will you be in to tea?"

"Yes," she promised, "I'll be in to tea." And, rather like a child herself, she thought: "Oh, I wish it were tea-time and this afternoon were over!"

Just before he went out for his afternoon walk, Betty brought him to her room to kiss her good-bye. Gwyneth was almost ready to go out herself, in a slim black suit with a great smoke fox collar.

"Good-bye, darling," she bent down to kiss the little, hatless, blue-clad figure. "Have a good walk."

"Good-bye. Have a good walk, too," Toby said politely. "You *will* be in to tea, won't you?"

"Oh yes."

"And can we have the chocolate biscuits with the cream in the middle?"

"I'll see we do."

"Thank you." He gave a little skip of pleasure, and ran back to Betty, who was smiling as she stood by the door, waiting for him.

"You're a very lucky boy," she remarked as they went off, and Toby said: "Yes, I'm a very lucky boy," very contentedly.

As she turned back to the glass to pull on her beautiful little black hat, Gwyneth thought:

"And I suppose she thinks I'm a very lucky woman, too." It would be impossible for Betty to suppose that her calm, beautiful, well-dressed employer had any serious cares in the world. Lots of money, a lovely home, a devoted, if stern, husband, and a dear little boy. What more could anyone want?

"Security," thought Gwyneth, as she went out of the flat. "Security—or what is any of it worth?"

She took a taxi to within walking distance of where Terry lived, in St. John's Wood. She would not take her own car and leave it outside, and she had a nervous disinclination to give Terry's address to any taxi-driver who might belong to the taxi-rank near her own home.

It was all very stupid and sordid, and she told herself grimly that she felt less respectable as—having seen the taxi drive away again—she turned down the road where Terry lived.

The 'rooms' of which he had spoken turned out to be the ground floor of a large and pleasant house, which had been converted into a garden flat. The manservant who admitted her either expected her or was quite used to his master having feminine visitors. Without any word of comment, he showed her into a well-furnished room, with large windows looking out on to a high-walled garden.

She sat down by one of the windows. She felt nervous, unhappily angry that she should have to be in this position, and she dreaded the coming interview. Never before had she had quite this feeling of angry shame. It was as though she were no more than a cast-off mistress, coming back to ask favours of a lover who had treated her badly.

When she heard his step outside, she stood up instinctively. And she hoped that she faced him with dignity rather than defiance as he came into the room.

"My dear Gwyneth, this is really delightful!"

Any other man would have been at least faintly abashed at the situation, but Terry came forward coolly and held out his hand without a trace of embarrassment.

She just touched his fingers with hers, and she didn't smile as she looked at him.

He hadn't changed. He hadn't changed one atom in all this time. How very lightly the years dealt with such easy-going scoundrels as Terry! She supposed he lived on the hearts and nerves and energy of other people—just as he lived on their money—and that was why time took no toll of him.

"Do sit down. I understand you wanted a really—intimate talk. And, if I may say so, Gwyneth, how very much lovelier you have grown."

"I came to speak about Paula," she said coldly and curtly. (Was it possible that she had once listened breathlessly to the slightest compliment this man chose to pay her?)

"Oh—Paula. Yes? And what about the charming Paula?"

A smile touched Terry's rather full lips, but it came nowhere near his eyes, she noticed. Those remained hard, bright and alert.

"Terry, I don't know that it's any good your hedging. You must know, as well as I do, that I can't possibly allow a young relation of mine to keep up a friendship with you —especially the kind of semi-secret friendship which you appear to have started."

She paused, but he said nothing, merely looked at her with those hard eyes and continued to smile.

"Well?" she said sharply.

"What, my dear?"

"What have you to say?"

"Nothing at all. I am waiting to hear how you intend to make the headstrong and romantic Paula break off this —semi-secret friendship."

"I have only to tell her a fraction of the truth and you know she would never look at you again."

"On the contrary, if you told her a fraction of the truth, she would never look at *you* again, because she would simply not believe you. No, no, my dear, you would have to tell Paula the *whole* truth. How does that strike you, eh?"

"If necessary, I would do it."

"And yet I feel, somehow, that Paula is not the girl to keep things entirely to herself. Now if your husband were to know—"

"My husband knows the whole story already," lied Gwyneth unflinchingly. "All he does not know is that you were the man."

For a second she saw indecision flicker in Terry's eyes, but it was gone almost at once.

"Very ingenious," he conceded, "but a damned lie."

"Are you quite sure you'd better risk putting that to the test?" Her voice was as hard as his now, and her eyes were like blue stones.

"The risk would be yours, Gwyneth. I *know* you're lying."

"How do you think you know?" she asked contemptuously.

"Because, if Evander Onslie had found that his wife had had dealings with another man, he would have left her. If he had found out before the marriage—well, my dear, the marriage would not have taken place. That's the long and the short of it. He's that sort of man."

Gwyneth sat perfectly still, her fingers locked together. It was strange and terrible to hear from Terry, of all people, the very words which hammered in her own brain day and night. He was right—Van was 'that sort of man'. Quite ruthless if he thought he had been deceived. Proud, honourable—and he adored her. If he were ever faced suddenly with the truth——

She raised her eyes slowly and looked at Terry. There was defiance in them—but she knew he had won the first round. "Well," he said pleasantly, "how do we stand now? As I see it, it will pay neither you nor me to start talking. What about a mutual agreement for silence?"

"No," Gwyneth said through rather dry lips. "No. I can't leave Paula unknowing and unprotected. We've got to come to some understanding, Terry."

"Have we?" He carelessly held out his cigarette-case to her, but she shook her head impatiently. "What have we got to understand?"

She shifted her ground slightly.

"Do you really imagine that I'm going to stand by doing nothing while you treat Paula as you treated me?"

"I've told you, Gwyneth—I don't really see what choice you have. In any case, Paula is rather a different proposition from you, as it happens."

"What do you mean by that?"

He shrugged deprecatingly.

"You may be very attractive now. In fact, you are—damned attractive. But you were distressingly sweet and colourless at seventeen. Paula, on the contrary, I find charming. I'll admit her charm is not diminished by the fact that she is the only child of wealthy parents. But I like Paula. I might even"—he smiled insolently, straight at her—"I might even settle down with her."

"*Marry*, do you mean?"

"An extreme measure, I agree, but not impossible."

"I thought you were married already—at least, once," she said bitterly.

"Certainly. Otherwise you, my delightful Mrs. Onslie, would be in the unpleasant position of still being married to me." He laughed as she whitened. "Fortunately for you, I *was* married when we had our little—escapade. But since then, I have had the—misfortune to lose my wife."

"In any case, it's immaterial——"

"I felt so, too."

"—I shouldn't allow Paula to have anything to do with you, legally or illegally," she finished, ignoring the cynical interruption.

He looked at her amusedly and slightly shook his head.

"I'm afraid you are perhaps just as childish as ever. At any rate, just as unable to realize when the tide is against you. Now listen, and I'll tell you the real facts." He leant forward, his elbows on his knees, his hands loosely clasped. "I admit that exposure would ruin me——"

"It might even put you in prison," she amended icily.

He shrugged.

"Very well. But it would also mean irretrievable ruin for you—not only socially but where your happiness with your husband is concerned. Incidentally, it would give a nasty knock to his happiness—so far as those proud "I'm-God-Almightly" men have feelings."

She wanted to tell him fiercely that Van had ten thousand times the feeling that *he* had. But it would be futile. And, anyway, he was speaking again.

"If you insisted on ruining us both—and I swear it should be a very complete ruin for you—I, at least, have a chance of getting away. A very good chance, since I am not without experience. But you, my dear, would have no escape. *Your* ruin would be in your own home"—he shrugged—"in your own heart, if you like, for I think you're very fond of that chilly husband of yours."

Gwyneth passed her tongue over her lips.

"Don't you see now that *you* are in no position to threaten *me?* If anything, the shoe is on the other foot—and it might be wiser of you to be a little more friendly to me," he added dryly.

Contempt, fear and anger looked at him from Gwyneth's blue eyes, but he didn't flinch. He had all the air of a gambler who holds the best cards.

105

For a long time there was silence in the room. Then she said in a low voice:

"Will nothing make you leave Paula alone?"

"I can't think of anything, Gwyneth. I'm really much too fond of her."

He laughed softly at the way she looked at him for that:

"How you do hate me!" He leant slightly further forward, and put his hand on her wrist, but she snatched her arm away with a proud, angry little movement. "And how much more attractive this way," he added amusedly. "No wonder even Evander Onslie fancied you."

She knew the fact that she winced angrily at his way of putting it only amused him further, but she managed to say steadily and coldly:

"We're getting rather far away from the point."

"Which is?"

"That naturally I shall do everything—*anything,* however unpleasant for myself—rather than see Paula's life ruined as mine was."

"You seem to have rebuilt it very satisfactorily, if I may say so," he observed carelessly. "It's not a bad thing to have Evander Onslie's cheque book to draw upon. But so far as Paula is concerned, I advise you—and I mean this with deadly seriousness, Gwyneth—I advise you not to interfere. The two people who would suffer most would not be Paula and myself. They would be you—and your precious Van."

She sprang to her feet at that. Partly because the truth of his words stung her unbearably, partly because she saw it was useless to continue and she might as well go.

He got to his feet too, but more slowly—smiling again slightly, because she was so lovely in her anger and despair.

"There doesn't seem to be anything else to say." She bit her lip sharply.

"There really doesn't, Gwyneth."

"I know you do hold all the best cards, but don't imagine I shall throw in my hand because of that."

"No? Well, I almost hope you don't, for you're so enchanting in a fighting mood. And there's no harm in your struggling for a while—unsuccessfully."

She swept that contemptuous, angry glance over him again; and turned to go without another word.

As she reached the door he spoke again behind her.

"There is one question I should like to ask—not entirely from idle curiosity."

"Well?" She turned reluctantly, her hand already on the door handle.

"Who was the child who answered the phone this morning, just before you spoke?"

Gwyneth went absolutely rigid. She knew she did. Then she could have cursed herself for betraying any dangerous concern, and she made every effort to cover the blunder.

"I can't imagine why you should be interested," she said dryly. "It was a little boy who is staying with us just now, if you must know."

"No connection of—your husband?"

"I'm afraid I don't know what you're getting at."

Did that cold blankness really sound as though she were annoyed and puzzled? she wondered. Or did it just sound as though she were feebly playing for time and trying to hide her agitation?

"I only wondered if it were some child you had—adopted?"

She knew he must be drawing a bow at a venture—and a pretty long bow, at that. Calling on the very last ounce of her self-control, she looked back at him with contemptuous calm.

"No," she said coldly, "he is not a child we have adopted. And the answer to your insinuation is "no", also."

And, turning away again, she went out of the room and out of the house.

Her knees were shaking under her so that she could hardly walk along the road, but she kept on telling herself that, at least, on the score of Toby there was no immediate reason to be afraid.

"I put him off there," she repeated over and over to herself, like a child afraid of the dark. "At least I put him off about that. He hasn't any real suspicions. He only made a malicious guess, and I didn't betray myself. Oh, I'm *sure* I didn't! He couldn't have noticed that first start, and I was absolutely convincing at the end. He *was* convinced. I know he was."

She found a taxi at last and, giving the address in an oddly husky voice that didn't sound much like her own, she got in and sank down thankfully on the seat. She felt drained and weary—rather as old people must feel when they had done something beyond their strength, she thought.

Now she wondered a little why she had ever bothered to go. She couldn't surely have been so absurd as to suppose that Terry would listen to any sort of appeal? And what he had said about her not being in a position to threaten was perfectly true.

He was the one who could threaten. He could threaten her whole happiness, and Van's and Toby's. Perhaps Toby didn't come into this immediately, but it was only one short step to him.

If Terry were going to visit their home—and since he absolutely refused to retreat, it was at least probable that she must let him—how could she hope to have Toby permanently? She couldn't explain him away indefinitely, and Terry was so cruelly, wickedly quick at guessing the truth. Already he had a faint suspicion, and she had perhaps crushed that only temporarily.

"I can't cope with things," she told herself distractedly. But she knew that she must. If she didn't, who else would?

The taxi stopped before she had found the answer to that.

Even tea with Toby had not the full savour today. She could smile at him and listen to his chatter and take pleasure in *his* pleasure, but nagging at her all the time was the thought of Paula—Terry, Terry—Paula.

Well, she had failed with the one. What was there to do but try the other? She must see Paula and tell her something—though God knew how much!—of her own wretched story. And she must risk Terry establishing for certain that she was behind any break there might be—and taking what revenge he pleased.

She telephoned to Paula as soon as Toby was in bed. Van was very late at the office that evening and so she was still alone and there was a chance to speak frankly, if necessary.

The first voice she heard was that of Paula's mother. Slow, heavy, dignified, and quite, quite impossible to hurry. No wonder such a lively spark as Paula was out of her element there!

Might she speak to Paula?

She might.

There was a pause and then Paula's voice—faintly bored and cross—sounded at the other end.

"Is that you, Paula?"

"Oh, Gwyneth dear!" came enthusiastically from the other end of the wire, as soon as Paula recognized the voice. "How are you after all your heroic adventures? I'm simply dying to see you."

"I'm quite all right again, thank you, except that I can't use my left arm for quite everything yet. But I rang up because I wanted to see you, too. Can you come along one afternoon soon?"

"I'd love to! The day after tomorrow?"

Gwyneth wanted to say 'Tomorrow,' and get it over, but she must not appear too pressing. And so she said that the day after tomorrow would do very well.

Somehow the intervening day and a half crawled away, while again Gwyneth hid her feelings as well as she could. She guessed that Van put down any quietness and pallor to her not having entirely recovered, and for that she was very thankful.

On the afternoon that she was expecting Paula, she sent Toby out with Betty again. He was very happy because he had found another little boy who played in the Park, and he was the proud owner of a puppy.

"Could I have a little dog, too?" he wanted to know, as Gwyneth buttoned up his blue coat.

"I don't know yet. We'll have to see, later on."

"I'd rather have a little lion, like the one at the Zoo."

"Well, I don't think we could manage that." She kissed him good-bye and handed him over to Betty.

Ten minutes later Paula arrived.

She was dressed in a beautiful shade of chestnut brown. Her short fur coat was a model and the diamond clasp in her hat was the real thing. Yes, Terry chose his opportunities well. 'Only child of wealthy parents' was right. It was stamped all over Paula.

"Dear Gwyneth!" She hugged Gwyneth with real affection. "I'm so glad to see you. Have you had a very rotten time?"

"No, not really. My arm and shoulder hurt a good deal at first, but that's over now, and I'm practically all right."

"And the little boy?"

"He's quite all right, too."

"No—I mean, you've got him here at the flat, haven't you?"

"Oh yes. He's out just now, but you'll see him later, at tea-time."

Paula tossed off her outdoor things and made herself comfortable.

"And how does Van take to his role of adopted parent?"

Gwyneth looked rather startled.

"We haven't actually adopted Toby, you know."

"No, I know. But, from the way Van spoke on the phone, I gather it's quite likely you will."

"Did he actually say anything about adoption?" Gwyneth felt a breath of excited happiness.

"I don't think he used the word." Paula wrinkled up her forehead thoughtfully. "But he spoke as though—what's his name?—Toby would more or less always be here."

Gwyneth smiled. There were *some* gleams of hope and happiness in the world. When the whole affair of Toby was going so well, it didn't seem possible that the other problem would remain insoluble and spoil everything.

"Paula," she said, summoning all her resolution, "I really wanted to talk to you about Terry Muirkirk."

"Yes, of course. I guessed as much."

Gwyneth twisted her wedding ring rather nervously on her finger.

"I'm afraid it isn't quite the sort of talk you were expecting, but——"

"Just a moment——" The interruption came rather sharply, and, looking up, Gwyneth saw that she was not the only one who was ill at ease.

"I think," Paula said slowly, "that it's much better if I'm quite frank. I know already about you and Terry."

CHAPTER SEVEN

"You—*know?*" Astonishment and terror and a strange relief struggled together in Gwyneth's heart. "But you can't know. Who told you?"

"Terry did."

"Terry? When?"

"Yesterday. I saw him yesterday afternoon," Paula said defiantly. "We had a long talk together."

"And he told you—about me?" She couldn't possibly imagine any motive for his doing that. If he wanted to betray her—ruin her life—Paula was not the confidante to choose. And if that were not his idea, what earthly point was there in his telling her? He would only completely alienate her.

Then was that it? Had Terry, by some improbable miracle, determined to do the decent thing and send Paula away?

She couldn't believe it. It was too simple—too wonderful. It couldn't be true! And yet, if it were, and Paula could now be relied on to keep silent, the horror was over. She could breathe again—live again—be happy again.

"Paula dear." She put out her hand and gently touched the girl's arm. "I'm sorry. Are you feeling very dreadful about it?"

"Oh no." Paula put her hand over Gwyneth's and pressed her fingers hard.

"You're not? I'm so terribly glad. I suppose the shock—"

"It wasn't a shock exactly, Gwyneth. I didn't imagine I was the first girl he'd been fond of. It was a bit of a blow to find it was actually someone I knew, of course. But you're happily married to Van now, so I know you must have got over it long ago. It would be stupid of me to brood over it now. It doesn't really make any difference."

She paused, but no answer greeted this extraordinary expression of tolerance.

Was the girl quite mad? Gwyneth wondered bewilderedly. Hadn't she any appreciation of right and wrong? Didn't she understand the despicable part which Terry had played? "It didn't make any difference," indeed! Then what, in heaven's name, *could* make any difference?

"Paula, I don't think you can possibly understand," Gwyneth began at last.

"Oh, yes I do. Really, I do. I know you must have felt awful at the time, poor pet. And of course, you thought he'd treated you very badly. But one does get over these things."

These things! How often did she suppose 'these things' happened?

And then suddenly Gwyneth went cold all over.

"What did Terry tell you exactly?" she asked in a queer, hard little voice.

"Oh, Gwyneth—" Paula looked uncomfortable. "Well, everything, I suppose."

"I want to know just what he said."

"But that can't do any good—I mean, it's rather embarrassing, Gwyn—for me as well as you."

"I want to know what Terry said," Gwyneth repeated inexorably. "I *must* know."

"Well, he explained about your meeting each other in the wood that time, in the beginning, and how you used to come after that and watch him sketching. He said you were rather a lonely girl, Gwyn, and—and very young for your age. He seems to have looked on you as a dear child more than anything else."

"Does he? Did he say so?"

"Yes. Yes, he did. He said you were awfully pretty and sweet, and he did get awfully fond of you. You mustn't think he feels it was all on your side. He does blame himself very much."

"For what?"

"For letting you get so fond of him without his realizing just where things were drifting."

"He used those words, too?" Her contempt and anger made the blood sing in her ears, and she knew she was flushing and paling by turns.

"Gwyneth, please don't distress yourself about it now. I know your pride must have had an awful jar at the time, but, really, lots of girls of seventeen are just as silly over men—write them letters and tell them they're in love with them, and that sort of thing—" Paula broke off, looking really unhappy, but Gwyneth said:

"Please go on."

"Oh well, then, if you *insist*. He told me how you—made some sort of declaration of love, and he found you were expecting you would marry him—considered you were more or less engaged to each other. I know you find it difficult to believe anything but the worst of him—or perhaps you understand better now you're older—but he was genuinely horrified, Gwyneth. He had no idea you were taking things so seriously. I suppose he forgot how girls of that age take everything seriously."

"Did he say that, too?" Gwyneth asked wearily.

"No. Oh no. That was just an observation of my own. You see, I do want you to know that I understand your side, too. I know myself what romantic and idiotic ideas I had only a year or two ago. I daresay I should have made just the same sort of ass of myself in the circumstances," she added generously. "Everything seems so big and important then and——"

"Seduction is not a small thing, at any age or by any standards," Gwyneth said with cold brutality.

"Gwyneth!" Paula's eyes went wide with horrified reproach. "How can you say such a wicked thing?"

Gwyneth gave a short, bitter laugh.

"Oh, he forgot that part, did he? He only told you the pretty little bits about meeting in the wood and wandering by the river—the parts you would recognize as the same sort of foolery that *you* had practised. He didn't speak about——"

"*Gwyneth!* Will you stop it!" Paula caught hold of her. "You're just getting hysterical with anger and jealousy. He said you would, but I didn't believe it. He said you'd make up almost any tale to poison me against him, but I didn't think you were so crazy."

Gwyneth was perfectly still now, contemplating with growing horror the completeness and simplicity of Terry's strategy. Paula scarcely noticed the quality of her silence. She ran on eagerly:

"Listen—I *know* he made you fond of him, and I *know* you don't want to forgive him and would like to spoil things for him, even now. But it isn't any good. Please, please—for your own dignity and pride—don't try to tell me these fantastic stories. You'll be so sorry afterwards. Don't you remember—it was really because you wouldn't control your jealous anger that everything took on such proportions before. For your own sake——"

"For the sake of my dignity and pride," repeated Gwyneth slowly. "Oh God, how funny!" And with a wretched little laugh she hid her face in her hands.

Paula sat there silent, gazing at her in dismay. At last she said unhappily:

"Gwyneth, I wish you wouldn't. You make me miserable and afraid."

"Afraid of what?" Gwyneth looked up quickly, with a faint hope that even now she might make Paula believe what she said. But the hope was short-lived.

"You make me afraid that you haven't really got over Terry. That you only married Van as a second best, and that now Terry has turned up again——"

"You needn't be afraid of anything like that," Gwyneth said quietly. "I am not a woman to hate easily, but I hate and despise Terry from the bottom of my heart. I know him for what he is—a heartless, mean, insolent scoundrel, and it is because of that that I have tried to save you. I don't know what he has said to you to make you feel that every word he utters must be true, while everything I say must be jealous invention. But he is lying, lying, lying all the time."

"I'm sorry, Gwyneth, but I simply don't believe you. Perhaps you half believe what you're saying yourself—I don't know. It's easy enough to imagine things when one is full of a sense of furious grievance. But you see, I know Terry and—yes, I love him. So, of course, I trust him, too."

Gwyneth looked back at Paula with a sort of cold despair.

"I suppose I should have spoken just like that if someone had tried to stop me," she said, half to herself. "What can I say to you, Paula? What can I say?"

Paula looked intensely uncomfortable.

"I wish you wouldn't say anything, Gwyn. It will only drive a wedge between us and spoil our friendship—and I should simply hate that. I don't know how you feel, but I don't in the least want to give up our friendship."

Gwyneth pushed back her hair wearily.

"I don't want to give it up, either," she said earnestly. She clung desperately to the one idea that she must not break off connection with Paula, or, indeed, the girl was lost. "Only—I suppose you hardly expect me to receive him here now?"

Paula didn't answer. She looked down at the hands that

were tightly clasped in her lap. And at the look of perplexity on her face, Gwyneth thought:

"But is even that rather wrong and stupid of me? If I don't receive him here, the child will see him in secret, then perhaps I shall be merely driving her further into his clutches."

Suddenly she decided to make one more effort.

"Paula, when I offered to help you—said I would try to make things easier so that you could introduce Terry to your mother—did I really strike you as the kind of woman who would make up lies about an—old flame, simply because I saw he liked another girl now? It surely isn't logical. It isn't even common sense."

Paula flushed again with genuine embarrassment, but Gwyneth saw she had not shaken her.

"Love and—and jealousy haven't anything to do with logic or common sense," she pointed out with dogged determination. "Besides, Terry said—— Oh, I don't know what good it is repeating these things! It only makes you judge poor Terry more and more hardly."

"I'd like to know, all the same, what poor Terry said about me."

Paula hesitated again, then, with a shrug, she gave in.

"He said that you are a very passionate girl, Gwyn, under all your surface coolness, and I can quite imagine that's true. He said you're very proud, too, and that you were terribly wounded in both your most sensitive feelings. And—and a proud and passionate woman never feels that things have been put right again until she's had some sort of revenge. It's true, you know. I can see what he means. And—and I don't blame you at all, Gwyneth. One can't help one's nature. He said that, too."

Gwyneth sprang to her feet.

"I give it up," she exclaimed bitterly. "I give it up. He has thought of everything and prepared every inch of the ground. There isn't anything else I can say. I only add picturesque touches to what he has told you to expect."

She walked restlessly across the room and back again, as though it were impossible to stay still any longer. As she did so Paula watched her—not in perplexity, but with a certain hopefulness. Gwyneth supposed grimly that Paula imagined she was making a great effort to overcome her personal feelings, and that her last outburst was merely a way of saving her pride.

Presumably she thought Gwyneth's generosity had conquered, because she said, rather timidly:

"Gwyneth, do you think—a little later—when you don't feel so badly—Terry *might* come? If you won't let him, I don't know what——"

"I don't know—— No, of course not. It's impossible." Gwyneth spoke almost harshly. Then, seeing the expression that came over Paula's face, she made as though to speak again. At that moment, she heard the front door open and the chattering voice of Toby sounded in the hall.

How soon the child's walk was over! Or perhaps their conversation had taken longer than she had supposed.

And what had she accomplished?

Nothing. She might as well have addressed herself to the wind.

For a brief, hysterical moment she wondered what effect it would have had if she had taken Toby by the hand and led him up to Paula with the words: "This is Terry's son. Terry's and mine."

But it was impossible!

As the door opened and Toby came expectantly into the room, she told herself fiercely: "There is nothing else that I can do." To Paula, she simply said in an undertone: "Don't say anything in front of the child. I'll speak about it later."

Toby ran to her, full of information about what he had seen on his walk. Pulling herself together, she introduced him to Paula, who also made an attempt to resume some appearance of calm.

"You're my Auntie Paula, aren't you?" Toby smiled at her in a friendly manner, quite unaware that he had interrupted a dramatic scene.

"Well, yes, I suppose I am, more or less." Paula grinned at him. Not quite the self-possessed and flashing smile she usually gave, but it seemed to satisfy Toby. And she spoke much more naturally as she added teasingly—"Where does that deep voice come from?"

"Here." Toby pressed his hand to his jersey.

"Well, I never heard such a deep voice."

"It's because I'm a man," Toby explained, with kindly indulgence for her ignorance, and Paula laughed.

Over tea, the presence of the little boy helped to ease the tension. He was very willing to be friendly to Paula, and he looked at her over the rim of his cup with a great deal of interest.

"Does Van usually come in to tea?" Paula asked.

Gwyneth shook her head.

"Not very often, but he may manage it today. I told him you were coming, and he said he would try not to be late."

"Van's very busy," observed Toby suddenly. "But he'll be in before I go to bed."

"Do you let him say that, Gwyn?"

Gwyneth looked rather nonplussed. Until now they had not really gone very carefully into the question of what Toby should call them. It was all very closely connected with whether or not Toby was to go back at the end of this holiday of his. In her heart she had hoped that if he came to live there permanently he would grow to look upon them as his parents. And, for the moment, he had not been told any definite way to address them.

"We haven't really settled anything yet."

"I suppose you're really waiting to see if the arrangement is going to be temporary or permanent?"

"Yes. One can't decide these things in a hurry," said Gwyneth, who could have decided that very moment, so far as she herself was concerned.

"No, no. The idea of a permanency."

"We haven't talked about it much yet, but I am hoping he will want it."

"You would like it very much yourself, wouldn't you?"

"Yes, very much."

"What?" asked Toby interestedly. "Will I like it, too?"

"I expect so." Gwyneth patted his head.

"Is it a secret?"

But Gwyneth said: "No, no," for she knew Toby's partiality for secrets, and she didn't want him to get the idea that there was something mysterious about his everyday life.

"There is Van," Paula said at that moment. "I heard his key in the door."

To her surprise, Gwyneth realized at once that Van was

117

not alone. He was speaking to someone as he came into the hall. It was unlike him to bring anyone home unexpectedly, especially when he knew Paula was coming, but——

And then she recognized the answering voice. She had heard it too recently to be mistaken, and in any case, it was stamped on her memory. There could not be any doubt about it—— For some horrible, inexplicable reason Van had brought Terry Muirkirk home with him.

Paula, too, had recognized the voice, but from her startled expression and the way she lost some of her colour, Gwyneth could see that this had not been any arrangement of hers.

The two men came into the room, Terry perfectly at ease, Van unaware that he was creating any sort of contretemps.

Gwyneth could not imagine how she faced the ensuing introductions, and somehow gave a fairly convincing impression of meeting Terry for the first time. His composure was really remarkable. His greeting implied just the right amount of courteous interest in meeting a connection of Paula's, and moreover, a connection whom he understood to be thoroughly sympathetic.

"Muirkirk happened to ring me up at the office this afternoon," Van was explaining. "As I knew Paula was coming, it seemed a very good opportunity for him to come along, too, and for us all to make each other's acquaintance."

Gwyneth could see that he believed, with some reason, that he had brought off a very neat little bit of strategy.

And Terry no doubt considered, for his part, that he had, too! He must have known about Paula's visit from something she had said the day before, and he had certainly chosen the time for his telephone call tactfully and well.

Toby, it seemed, was anxious not to be overlooked in the round of introductions.

"Hello, Van." He beamed up at Van engagingly.

"Hello, young man." Something like pleasurable amusement gleamed in Van's eyes, and he picked the little boy right up off his chair. "Who said you could call me that?"

"It's your name, just as my name's Toby," Toby asserted firmly.

"One of my names. Can you say "Mr. Onslie?" "

But Toby shook his head and said: "It's too hard."

Van laughed and kissed him with so much real tenderness and such a complete absence of embarrassment that Paula looked quite astonished.

"Who is this?" Terry asked agreeably, and in spite of all her efforts to keep calm, Gwyneth found that she was trembling so much that she had to sit down again. Otherwise she would have fallen.

"This is Toby." To Gwyneth's excited fancy it seemed that there was something very much like pride in Van's tone as he said that: "He is a great friend of ours, and he is staying with us just now."

"How do you do, Toby?" Terry looked at the child curiously, and held out his hand with a smile.

Toby solemnly placed his hand in Terry's, but for some unknown reason his ready smile was missing. He looked at Terry very seriously indeed.

There was something very painful to Gwyneth in the drama of this meeting between Toby and his father. No one in the room had any idea of the significance of it except herself, and for her, the significance was almost too heavy to bear.

As it was, a spasm of acute fear shot through her as Terry jerked her to the surface of things again with the apparently casual:

"Isn't this the little boy whom your wife rescued from the fire?"

"Yes." Toby was eager to explain the distinction which was his. "I was nearly burnt up."

"Well, you don't seem much the worse for it," Terry said with a laugh.

"No," Toby said, and he exchanged an extraordinarily sweet smile with Gwyneth, as though he had known all along that she would not let any real harm happen to him.

"Wasn't it down at Greystones Orphanage?" Terry asked pleasantly.

"Yes." Van's reply was just a trifle curt. Perhaps he saw no necessity to emphasize the fact that Toby came from an orphanage. Terry immediately left the subject—only

119

allowing his eyes to rest on Gwyneth with an interested smile that sent cold waves of fear over her.

The conversation became general after that. Toby remained close beside Van. In fact, after a few minutes, he was lifted on to Van's knee, and there he remained for the rest of the meal.

Still under the impression that he was improving a very satisfactory situation, Van politely pressed Terry and Paula to remain with them for the evening, and—helpless to alter things—Gwyneth had to listen with a fixed smile of approval while both of them accepted with heartfelt satisfaction.

"You haven't seen much of each other since you left Belgium, have you?" Van said, with real consideration. "I've no doubt you have plenty to say to each other."

"Oh——" Terry seemed slightly amused. "You know all about the beginning of our friendship, then?"

"Yes, I explained," Paula interrupted quickly, "Van and—and Gwyneth are the kind to whom you can explain."

Terry turned to Van with a laugh.

"I'm afraid Paula worries rather unduly over the fact that her people and my people didn't know each other—and all that sort of thing. Suitable connections weren't much to the fore when we struck up an acquaintance."

"Oh, I don't worry," Paula said with a little toss of her head. "It's only that I happen to have rather stuffy parents."

"Which is sometimes a rather fortunate thing," Gwyneth put in curtly. It was said so abruptly that it sounded almost rude, and there was a moment of disconcerted silence.

Ironically enough, it was Terry—she knew he was enjoying himself—who smoothed over the awkward moment.

"As a matter of fact, Mrs. Onslie is perfectly right in theory," he remarked. "But all the same"—he smiled straight at her—"I'm glad she has agreed that a little relaxation is permissable in my case."

At that moment Gwyneth could willingly have killed him, and she welcomed the diversion which covered her feelings when Betty came to take Toby off to bed.

Toby was reluctant to withdraw from the party, but Gwyneth, almost superstitiously anxious to see him removed from Terry's notice, was absolutely firm.

"I'm not tired. I shan't be able to go to sleep for ages," Toby repeated convincingly several times. But the age-old arguments met with no success.

"You'll feel quite different when you're in bed, darling," Gwyneth assured him gravely. "And I'll come and kiss you good night."

He bade a rather lingering farewell to both guests— Paula very much amused and intrigued by his simple strategy, Terry watching him with a closeness of attention which his affable smile did nothing to hide. It brought a tight feeling round Gwyneth's throat, and made her wonder if she had gone absurdly pale.

When Toby had gone at last, Terry turned to his hostess with an air of amused interest.

"What a charming child. You certainly chose a very attractive little fellow to rescue."

Somehow Gwyneth smiled.

"He is a dear, isn't he?" she agreed formally.

"I suppose it was the fact that you *had* rescued him which made you sufficiently interested to have him here?"

"Oh no." It was Van who spoke now, apparently a little displeased at the idea that they would have been stampeded into their decision by nothing more than a sentimental impulse. "Toby and my wife were great friends before that."

"Indeed?" Terry looked surprised and even more interested. "You quite often go to Greystones, then, Mrs. Onslie?"

"I had been there before," Gwyneth said rather faintly. "My husband is a trustee of the place, you know."

"Toby took a great fancy to her almost at once and insisted on being friends," Van explained. "As you will have noticed," he added with a tolerant little smile, "he is a young gentleman who is very difficult to turn from his purpose."

"I think he's a pet," Paula said. "He's killing when he calls you "Van"."

"I dare say. But we must put a stop to that, I'm afraid."

"Yes, I suppose so. But "Mr. Onslie" sounds ridiculous from that scrap. You could make it "Uncle Van"."

"We could, of course. Van's tone didn't really invite further discussion, but Paula hardly noticed that.

121

"On the other hand, if he stayed with you always, I suppose you'd want him to regard you more or less as parents."

There was a moment of startled silence. Van looked across at his wife, to find her watching him with half-scared eagerness.

"I suppose," he said slowly, "we should." And he saw her lashes come down and her mouth tremble slightly.

"Really?" Terry looked surprised and interested again. "Were you seriously thinking of adopting him?"

Van frowned very slightly. He seemed to find Terry's interest just a little too personal.

"Well, of course, we hadn't come to any real decision about it." He got up from his seat and strolled over to light a cigarette. When he sat down again it was on the arm of his wife's chair. "At the same time, I think both of us are going to find it hard to part with him. Don't you agree, Gwyn?"

Gwyneth nodded. She was quite unable to speak. And when she felt Van unobtrusively take her hand in his and clasp her fingers warmly, she knew he was aware of how moved and happy he had made her. It made up a little for the last dreadful hour or two.

"I think it's very courageous of you." Terry's voice held just the right note of admiring interest. "Adopting a child is always something of a risk—particularly if you know nothing at all of the child's antecedents. And I suppose you don't, in this case?"

"Nothing at all," agreed Van coldly and smoothly.

At the question, Gwyneth had thought that she must faint. But when Van took away all necessity for her to answer—and took it away so coolly and positively—she regained her composure again.

What would she do without him? Even without remotely guessing at her agitation of mind, he seemed by instinct to say the very things that would help her in her predicament.

It was that, and that alone, which sustained her for the rest of that dreadful evening.

When at last they were going, Paula drew Van aside to give him some message from her father in connection with his business, and for a few minutes, Terry and Gwyneth were practically alone together.

122

"I have to thank you for a very pleasant evening, Mrs. Onslie." His dark blue eyes full of amusement and that suggestion of insolence. "I hope, through Paula, to see a good deal of you and your husband."

"That's very kind of you." No effort could make her voice anything but very cold. "But we don't go out a great deal. My husband is such a very busy man, you know."

"Of course. And no doubt you will be very busy, too, if you take on this little boy permanently."

She met his eyes squarely, but she supposed he saw her swallow nervously.

The next moment he had taken her hand, whether she liked it or not, and kissed it lightly. As he straightened up again his eyes met hers once more and he said very quietly:

"I think we may both feel proud of him. He is a delightful child."

Then he turned away.

"Ready, Paula? Let me give you a lift. I have my car outside."

She had to say good-bye to Paula then, and to try to return her friendly hug with a reassuring one which should convey: "All right. We're still friends, of course."

Van went with them into the hall. There were a few final remarks exchanged, while Gwyneth, alone in the room, tried to rub some colour into her cold cheeks. Then the door closed and Van came back.

She was sitting by the fire by then, holding out her hands to the warmth, so that she could keep her face turned away for a few moments longer.

Her conventional: "How much colder it has grown," sounded steady, so steady that it helped to bolster up her failing courage. And gradually it was borne in on her that she could not have looked and sounded as awful as she felt, because he evidently didn't know that anything was wrong.

"How did you like him?" Van asked casually as he reached for a cigarette.

"What, Terry—Muirkirk?" She added the second name just in time.

"Yes."

With some half formed idea of doing something even now, she turned to face her husband.

"To be perfectly frank, I didn't like him at all, I think he's detestable."

"Do you really?" Van looked genuinely surprised. "But why, quite? Apart from a certain amount of curiousity about Toby—and I suppose that was natural—he made himself very pleasant, I thought."

"I think he's a rotter—and I wouldn't trust him an inch."

Van leaned his elbow on the mantelpiece and looked down at her.

"But you still don't say why, my dear."

"It's—it's an instinctive dislike and mistrust. I—can't explain it. Women do have these "hunches" more often than men, I think."

Her husband shrugged slightly.

"Perhaps you're a little prejudiced by the way he met Paula."

"No, I'm not. Really, I'm not, Van. But I'm terribly distressed to think of her having anything to do with him. I'm *sure* he won't be any good to her. She's rather an artless girl, in spite of all her superficial confidence. And she's no judge of people at all. With a clever scoundrel she'd be all at sea."

"I think you're letting your anxiety run away with you, Gwyn." Van spoke quite kindly, but a little as though he thought her unreasonable. "Muirkirk hasn't done anything at all to suggest that he's a scoundrel—clever or stupid, come to that. And I think, when a man's only too eager to meet a girl's relations and make himself agreeable, there isn't much wrong."

"That might just be his cleverness."

Van laughed at that and came and put his arm round her.

"You're nervous because we've more or less condoned this secret friendship and made ourselves responsible for introducing him into Paula's home, aren't you? But I really don't think you need worry. As I told you before, Paula is very well able to look after herself and, speaking objectively, I should say Muirkirk is a nice enough fellow."

He didn't know, of course. He *couldn't* know. It made her sick to think how helpless she was.

"I don't know that Muirkirk matters very greatly to us,

124

in any case," Van said after a moment. "There was something else mentioned this evening that is far more interesting to us personally."

"Oh"—she looked up at him—"you mean Toby?"

He nodded, his smiling eyes on her face.

"Van, would you really like us to keep him always?—actually adopt him."

"Yes," her husband said slowly, "I can honestly say I should. In theory, of course, I never thought of our doing such a thing. But he is so dear and affectionate. One couldn't do anything but—love him." He brought the word out with the faintest embarrassed hesitation. "Besides, it would make you so happy, wouldn't it?"

"Oh, *so* happy, Van— *so* happy!"

"Would it take away that sad, anxious look from your eyes?"

"Van! Do I really look sad and anxious?"

"Sometimes."

"I'm ashamed of myself," she exclaimed. "When I have the best husband in the world and—and everything to make me happy, how awful that I still contrive to look a misery!"

He laughed and kissed her.

"You're not a misery, darling. But when you want a thing very much, it is difficult not to give the fact away to someone who loves you."

She didn't know whether that comforted or frightened her. It was sweet of him to anticipate her every want—but what more might one perhaps 'give away' to someone who loved one?

"You're so good to me, Van. Much too good, I think sometimes."

"Then that's very silly of you," he said gently. "Don't you know what pleasure it is for me to be able to give you anything you want?"

She thought how indescribably different he was from Terry. But then, of course, he thought her perfect. Whereas Terry—base creature that he was himself—knew also the depths to which she had sunk. No wonder he secretly despised her and thought her of not very much worth.

"Then it's settled?" Van's voice said quietly.

"Oh, Van, just as simply as that?"

"Well, do you want to give more thought to it?"

"Not—really." But that was not entirely true, because she knew she ought to give more thought to it—ought to try to work out the tangle of how this would affect Terry —how Terry, with his latest dangerous discovery, would decide to act—whether it simplified or complicated things.

But she couldn't work it out. And she couldn't hesitate any more, either.

"It's wonderful, Van dear. You think of everything and you do it in the nicest possible way."

He laughed, but she knew how pleased he was.

"Nothing else in the world to worry about?" he wanted to know.

"Nothing," Gwyneth said firmly as she kissed him.

Afterwards, when she was lying awake in bed, thinking over the events of the evening, she half convinced herself that there was *not* so much to worry about as she had supposed.

Perhaps one grew almost used to living on the edge of a volcano, or, perhaps, it was just that the immediate terrible crisis was past and there was bound to be a sense of relief But—whatever the reason—as she lay there listening to Van's quiet, even breathing, she felt her nervous tension relaxing, and very timidly her mind began to explore the less terrible possibilities in the present situation.

At least Toby was to be safely hers. Van wished it—for her sake and also because, as she had hoped, the child had made his own appeal.

To be sure, Terry had guessed Toby's real identity, and nothing she could say now would shake his belief in that. She clenched her hands again nervously at the thought. But, on the other hand, he stood to gain nothing and lose everything if he disclosed what he knew. The possibility of his betraying her had been a powerful threat in his hands —but only to be used in revenge, if she were responsible for spoiling his own plans.

And it seemed she *could* not be responsible. Paula simply would not listen to what she had said.

She had done her best, she assured herself. She had honestly done her best. Short of telling Paula the absolute truth and ruining the lives of Van and herself and Toby, there was nothing more that she could do. Paula must find

126

out for herself now. All that Gwyneth could do was to keep in close touch with her and try to anticipate any specially foolish step that she might take.

Gwyneth thought of what Terry had said about marrying Paula. At the time she had paid it no more than a contemptuous moment of notice, but now she recalled it more seriously.

He had said the dreadful woman who had been his wife was dead. With a shiver, Gwyneth wondered in what dreary, loveless, sordid surroundings she had met her end. Terry would not be much comfort to one at a time like that.

But now he was free, and the brutal truth was that not only his inclinations but also his material interests would be served by marrying Paula. Gwyneth knew that would make a great difference in Terry's behaviour. It was not impossible that, while conscience would never regulate his conduct, self-interest might.

She could not think without a shudder of Paula really married to Terry, and yet he would not be the first scoundrel to become a fairly honest man simply because honesty paid best. Paula would find out in time, of course, that he was not all she thought, but she might never have reason to find out his worst depths.

The qualities which fascinated her now might really continue to do so if Terry never had reason to tear the veil from her eyes himself.

"I'm trying to make it all sound sugary and touched with the happy-ever-after wand," thought Gwyneth guiltily. "But it could be something like that. It *could* be. God grant it is!"

She fell asleep at last, worn out with the strain of all that she had passed through, and yet comforted by the thought—illogical but persistent—that the worst was over.

CHAPTER EIGHT

ODDLY enough, at breakfast the next morning Toby looked up suddenly and said:

"When do I have to go?"

"Go where, dear?" She was putting milk on his porridge and Van was absorbed in his morning post.

"Away from here. Back—there."

She thought how sad it was that he had never learned to use the word 'home'. And then she remembered—in future he would learn the word and it would mean her home.

"How would you like to stay here for a very long time?"

"With you?"

"Yes."

"And Mr. Van?"

Gwyneth laughed. "Yes."

Toby stared hard at his porridge, and she watched him rather anxiously. Presently, to her astonishment and dismay, she saw two tears begin to roll down his cheeks. She had never seen Toby cry before, not even when he had been frightened by the fire, and the sight moved her deeply.

"Darling, what is it?" She put her arms round him.

"I don't want to go *at all*," Toby sobbed. "I don't want to have white soap and no chocolate biscuits and not see you and Mr. Van any more."

"Oh, Toby dear!" She was terribly touched, not any the less because she came third on the list. "You shan't ever go away. I promise you shan't. We'll keep you always and always."

"Will you?"

"Of course. We want you."

He looked round her at Van, who had put down the letter he had been reading and was watching this scene with a complicated expression.

Toby scrambled down off his chair suddenly and ran to Van. It was odd how he always seemed to sense that, in some way, the last word lay with Van.

"Do you want me always, too?" he asked anxiously. And Van caught him up and kissed him as affectionately as Gwyneth had done.

"I wouldn't part with you," he said, "for all the green soap and chocolate biscuits in the world."

It didn't seem that there would be any great complications in the matter of making Toby theirs for ever. Van offered to go down to Greystones and see Dr. Kellaby himself, but Gwyneth said:

"I think I'd like to come with you. Mrs. Kellaby was so very kind to me. I should like her to know how happily it has all turned out."

So they both went down to Greystones, and though it was a very cold day—much, much colder than either of the days when she had made the journey before, Gwyneth felt warm all through. And the warmth had little to do with the fur coat she was wearing.

"I *thought* it would turn out like that," Mrs. Kellaby declared. "If we hadn't got something like ninety-five others left, I don't think I could bear to part with Toby, myself."

"He is a dear child," Dr. Kellaby said, "and a good child. On one side, at least, he comes from excellent people. That I do know. The mother was a girl of very good family."

"Was she?" Van looked only slightly interested.

"Was she?" Gwyneth repeated, and felt herself go cold all over.

"Yes. I didn't know the full circumstances of the story, but I think it must have been the old story of a rather innocent sort of girl being led away by a bounder. She was very young, I understand. The girl's mother brought Toby here. A most unusual type of woman. A great deal of surface charm, I remember, and yet somehow unlikeable. A very cold-hearted woman, I should say."

Gwyneth sat there dumb. It was impossible either to stop the story being told or to make any suitable comments. And then, as though it were a horrid dream in which she could only watch helplessly, unable to wake, she heard Dr. Kellaby say:

"The records are very meagre, I'm afraid. It was quite a mysterious case, but I expect, since you are taking Toby permanently, you would like to see what information we *have* got."

He had already risen and begun to unlock the safe in his study when Van spoke again.

"Do you know, Kellaby, I almost think I prefer *not* to see anything there is. I don't know how my wife feels about it, but personally, I feel that the less we associate Toby with any other actual people, the more he will seem like our own. What do you think, Gwyn?"

With a tremendous effort, Gwyneth snatched at this extraordinary, last-minute reprieve.

"I agree entirely," she said with perhaps a little more

129

fervour than was strictly necessary. "I—I feel Toby *is* ours. I don't want to think of him as—as having any people except us. We shall be bringing him up as our own child. In fact, I want him to regard us as his father and mother. Don't you, Van?"

She was speaking rather too quickly and breathlessly, she knew, but Van didn't seem to notice that.

"Yes," he agreed, "that's exactly how I feel. I think we can leave it at that."

"It's unusual for adopters to feel as you do," Dr. Kellaby said with a smile, "but I've known it happen before. And, as a matter of fact, I'm not at all sure that it isn't the wisest way in the end."

"I'm certain of it," Van said firmly. And, scarcely able to believe her good fortune, Gwyneth realized she was safely past what was probably the last dreadful danger point.

Even when they were alone again in the car on the way home, Van didn't seem inclined to speak of Toby's meagre past history. It was Gwyneth herself, unable to feel that the whole question was so simply closed, who referred to it.

"I think it is really the best way to let Toby come to us as quite a little unknown. I shouldn't have thought of being so strong-minded as to refuse to see the records, but since you did it, I am very glad to have it so."

"He feels more like our own child that way," Van said.

"Ye-es." Something in the way he said that reminded her very strongly of their conversation on this same road months ago, when he had refused to consider the idea of their interesting themselves in Toby.

"Van——" He glanced at her and smiled, so that she instinctively moved a little closer to him. "I don't know whether there is any need for me to put this into words, but—please don't ever feel that Toby is *instead* of a child of our own. I should love it if one day we did have one. I—I'm so afraid you'll feel that in a way I've cheated you."

"And I'm so glad," Van said, "that we've really decided to adopt Toby."

"But why? I mean, why specially at this moment?"

"Because you say "thank you" so sweetly. No one ever says it as you do, Gwyn. And—I know—you've been sitting there wondering what you could give me that would please me as much as this has pleased you, weren't you?"

"I—suppose so." She smiled.

"Well, I want Toby as much as you do, darling, but I hope—just as you do—that one day there will be another baby, too. One thing is certain—there shall never be the slightest scrap of difference made between them. We owe that to Toby for his having given us so much happiness."

She didn't answer that with anything beyond a smile, but it was so tremulously happy that it was more eloquent than words. She sat very still beside him after that, her eyes brilliant and tender. For Van had said, in so many words, that her child should be regarded as *his* child.

There followed an amazingly happy week or two for Gwyneth. She could really allow herself to revel in the happiness of having her child in her home, and she and Van taught him, with very little trouble, to regard them and speak of them as his parents.

"I never had a mummy and daddy before," he informed them. "We didn't have any at Greystones." But he gave them to understand, in no uncertain way, that he was very well satisfied with the two who had fallen to his lot now.

When it came to writing home to tell her parents of what they had done, Gwyneth wondered how she was going to put it to them. Her mother, of course, could scarcely be kept from guessing the real truth, but Gwyneth decided it was best not to commit any real information to paper.

In the end, she addressed the letter to both her parents, and carefully made it the kind of letter which any daughter might have addressed to her parents when she had quite unexpectedly decided to adopt a child who had no connection with her at all.

Almost by return of post, they replied to her—separately. And each reply was quite characteristic.

Her father wrote four pages in his beautiful, flowing handwriting, expatiating upon the happiness and responsibility of having a little child in one's home. He said he was slightly surprised that, at such an early date, they had decided to take a homeless waif (disregarding the excellent conditions at Greystones) into their home, rather than wait for the gift of a child of their own. But, in an agreeable finale, he came to the conclusion that his daughter's heart was 'large enough to shelter this little unfortunate' as well as any children that might come to them. "And I have," he added, "the greatest confidence in Van's considered judgment in this, as in most other matters."

Then Gwyneth turned to her mother's letter.

Following Gwyneth's own admirable caution, Mrs. Vilner gave not the slightest hint of having read anything into her daughter's letter which had not been expressly set down there, and every word of her own short reply could be read with equal safety by either Gwyneth or Van.

I am sure you both know your own minds best (she wrote), and so it would be quite absurd of other people to generalize about adopted children versus one's own, and that sort of thing. I suppose Toby is the child to whom you gave the jug, and so I take it the liking for him was not just a momentary impulse.

He sounds a very nice child, and as soon as possible I shall take the opportunity of spending a day or two in London in order to make his acquaintance myself. I don't know that anything will persuade your father to come, too—I doubt it, for you know how hard it is to drag him away from his beloved books—but perhaps, later on, you might like the idea of spending Christmas or New Year down here, and he and Toby can meet each other then.

Gwyneth smiled slightly as she read the letter. It was a model of what a tactful, affectionate parent should write, and the kindly, half rueful reference to her studious father was perfectly in character. No one could have visualized from that letter the woman Dr. Kellaby had described as 'very charming but somehow unlikeable'. Mother really did these things splendidly.

However, although she might give no sign of having read between the lines, there was no doubt in Gwyneth's mind that she had done so. And when, a very little while later, Mrs. Vilner wrote to say she was coming to London for a day or two, Gwyneth steeled herself for rather disagreeable explanations and, perhaps, a certain amount of disapproval.

She scarcely minded. Her extreme happiness with Toby nowadays made her more confident, and less inclined to dread the future.

The bond between Van and the child was a very real one by now. It was not that Van just tolerated him because she wanted him and he was a good child anyway. He would often take a great deal of time and trouble to satisfy Toby's many inquiries, and if he were so late home that Toby had gone to bed—as sometimes happened—he always inquired after the child the first thing, and smiled rather indulgently over whatever she had to tell of the day's happenings.

Of Paula she had not seen very much during the last few weeks. Gwyneth tried very earnestly to keep in touch with her, and once or twice there had been quite long telephone conversations, but it was almost impossible, of course, for relations not to be slightly strained.

She gathered that Terry visited the house at Norbury now, and apparently he had made a good impression on the parents.

It looked as though Terry meant to follow a conventional and respectable path so far as Paula was concerned. And, in that case—odd though it seemed—possibly Paula would be happier with him than with anyone else.

"One *can't* be wise for other people," Gwyneth thought. "It's difficult enough to be wise for oneself. And I suppose interference is more often harmful than helpful."

And so, for the moment, she left it at that.

When her mother arrived it was early afternoon. Van, of course, was not at home, and Toby was out with Betty. So there was an excellent opportunity, as her mother said, for a really long talk.

Mrs. Vilner settled herself comfortably on the settee and looked at her daughter penetratingly.

"Well, no doubt it's an unnecessary question," she began, "but I suppose this child is your own?"

Gwyneth pressed her lips together.

"Yes. Of course."

"Gwyneth, for a timid girl, you really do the most wildly rash things."

"Do I?"

"You know you do. I take it that Van hasn't the slightest idea of the truth?"

"Of course not. Not the slightest."

"Well, my dear, don't you ever *think* what sort of danger you're running? I don't know anybody else on earth who would venture to adopt her own child under the nose of her unsuspecting husband."

"The idea was Van's, as a matter of fact," Gwyneth said coldly, and there was a gleam of amused admiration in her mother's eyes at that.

"Really, Gwyneth, I begin to think I underestimate your cleverness," she exclaimed. "How did you manage that?"

"It wasn't "managing", exactly." Gwyneth frowned. "Van saw how terribly I wanted Toby and—and he really loves giving me anything that will give me pleasure, you know. Almost at once, too, he began to find Toby very attractive, himself, and now he loves him dearly."

"And he didn't suspect a thing at any point? How dense men can be!"

"But, Mother, why on earth *should* he suspect, when you come to think of it coolly? Who would think of anything quite so fantastic—especially in connection with his own wife? It's hard enough to believe such things happen to other people. It's almost impossible to think of them in one's own life. Sometimes I can hardly believe it myself," she added sadly.

"No? Well, in Van's position I should certainly have looked for some sort of explanation when a young woman, only just married, conceived an inexplicable desire to adopt some child she had seen only twice."

"It wasn't quite like that." Gwyneth spoke in a low voice. "And then I think he thought I was very deeply affected by the scene when Toby was nearly burnt. It was after that that he seemed to take it almost as a foregone conclusion that we should have him. I was at the orphanage. ill, for some time, you remember, and, of course, I saw a lot of Toby. So did Van. We—we both grew fond of him. It followed fairly naturally. First we had him home on a visit, and then—then we couldn't part with him."

"You mean *you* couldn't."

"No, I think Van felt that way too. Anyway, it was he who actually suggested the adoption." She was faintly surprised to realize that both times the suggestion *had* come from Van.

"And so now everything is satisfactorily settled?"

"Well, yes, I think it is." Gwyneth wished her mother wouldn't smile in that slightly scornful way, which seemed to suggest that she could scarcely believe her daughter was so ingenuous as to suppose everything *was* all right.

"And you're not afraid of Van finding out?"

"Why should I be—now?" Gwyneth's voice was slightly defiant.

"I don't know, my dear. You know best how well you have covered your tracks. But, in your place, I should far rather have left the child where he was than risk the absolute holocaust there would be if Van ever did find out."

Gwyneth was silent.

"Perhaps the risk is small—I hope it is—but, though I am not a nervous woman, I must admit I should be haunted by the thought that it could happen, and that there would be remarkably little left in life if it ever did happen."

Gwyneth shivered slightly. It was very true, of course.

"I don't think Van would choke you exactly, because he's a little too self-contained for murder, but I can't imagine he would stop very far short of it."

"And I don't think you know Van particularly well if you can talk like that! Are you trying to frighten me—"

"No. But by the very insanity of the risk you have taken, you show that you have practically no appreciation of danger. I'm trying to warn you to be doubly, trebly careful."

"You need not bother." Gwyneth spoke very curtly. "I know the risks well enough. I know I'm living on the edge of a volcano. But I can't help it. I couldn't—I wouldn't—give up Toby. If I can have him only by risking all this—well then, I'm risking it. Do you suppose I don't hate it? Do you suppose I don't wonder every morning if I shall reach the end of the day without ruin overtaking me? But it's no good. It's that or losing Toby. I can't do without him now——"

"You did without him very well for five years," her mother reminded her dryly.

"I know. But then I thought he was dead. That's a very different matter. When I saw him and knew him for the dear, odd, loving little personality that he is, I couldn't go on, knowing always that he was "an institution child", that he had no home, that he thought me a dear, pretty visitor who only came once every few months, but whom he wanted to follow about everywhere. I *loved* him, Mother. I couldn't leave him then."

"Well, my dear, it's your own life you're playing with, of course, so the whole thing is really your own business. It might not seem so dangerous with another type of man. But with Van——" She broke off and shrugged.

"Van can be much gentler than you imagine," Gwyneth said in a low voice.

"Very likely. But I don't think you would find his gentleness much in evidence if he ever found out about your escapade."

Again Gwyneth was silent. If only Mother wouldn't keep on putting her own fears into words!

"Gwyneth." Mrs. Vilner spoke again in a rather different tone.

"Yes?"

Gwyneth glanced up to find her mother frowning thoughtfully.

"Is it your intention—yours and Van's—to put through a legal adoption, by and by? Not just let him stay on indefinitely, I mean, without putting things on an official basis."

"I'm sure it's Van's intention to have a formal adoption, though, to tell the truth, we haven't gone into everything very closely yet. We went down to the orphanage, of course, and explained to the Kellabys what we wanted to do. They were extremely kind and helpful, but they said—Dr. Kellaby said there was very little known about Toby. He only mentioned two things——"

"And they were?" Mrs. Vilner spoke really sharply that time.

"That he understood the mother was a girl of good family. And I'm afraid, Mother, that he didn't like you."

"Oh——" Mrs. Vilner laughed shortly, "I suppose that was the Superintendent I interviewed. I had forgotten the name. I remember now—I didn't like him either. He had some absurd theory about it being best to leave the child with——" She broke off. "Well, anyway, it doesn't matter now. It's years ago." But Gwyneth saw that whenever Dr. Kellaby had said rankled still.

"Anyway, I'm glad," Gwyneth said slowly, "that Dr. Kellaby was human enough to think that—that Toby's mother should have been allowed to keep him. For I suppose that was what you were going to say."

Mrs. Vilner didn't answer, and Gwyneth rather thought she could imagine the scene—Mother's 'surface charm' breaking down under the absurd suggestion that one should behave with something like real heart.

After a moment her mother spoke again.

"What happened when they looked up the child's registration, or whatever it is?"

"Nothing. Or rather, it never happened. Van was absolutely determined that we should make no investigations into Toby's very meagre little past. He felt very strongly that the less he knew about the—the real parents, the more he would feel Toby was his own."

"Good heavens!" Mrs. Vilner laughed incredulously. "You certainly have the most incredible luck, my dear. Either that or—— But no. That isn't possible, of course."

"What?" Gwyneth asked.

But Mrs. Vilner only shook her head. She still had a last word of warning for her daughter, however.

"Be very careful when you come to the actual legal adoption, my dear, because I believe some attempt is always made to obtain the consent of one at least of the real parents."

Gwyneth paled.

"Are you sure?"

"No, not absolutely. They may dispense with that in the case of a child taken from an orphanage. I suppose they would have to, in some cases, where really nothing at all was known. But I wish you had thought of some of these pitfalls before you insisted on this crazy plan of having the child."

"If I had thought about them, I should never have had him," Gwyneth retorted harshly. "I couldn't afford to count the cost and lose my nerve before I had even begun. As it is, I must face each risk as it comes along."

Mrs. Vilner shrugged.

"That is the counsel of almost insane rashness. It means you're not even prepared for an emergency, Gwyn."

"Against what emergency *can* I prepare?"

Mrs. Vilner raised her eyebrows.

"Are you never afraid, for instance, that the child's own father might turn up?"

Gwyneth looked at her mother with a certain cold defiance.

"He *has* turned up," she said, at least as dryly as her mother had spoken.

Mrs. Vilner sprang to her feet, her astonishment and dismay galvanizing her into action.

"He *has*—and you sit there doing nothing! Are you quite crazy, Gwyneth? Have you no sense of danger at all?"

Gwyneth smiled—a little as her mother might have smiled in other circumstances.

"Do sit down again, Mother. How very odd—I seem to remember Aunt Eleanor once saying very much the same thing to you—about having no sense of danger. I must have inherited it from you, I think."

"You certainly did not." Her mother dropped back into her seat again, a little annoyed at having betrayed quite so much agitation. "I'm not a coward, but at least I don't invite danger and then sit back waiting for disaster to happen."

"Well, I didn't invite danger, if by danger you mean Terry. He simply came back into my life, whether I liked it or not—paying some doubtful sort of court to a young cousin of Van's."

"Good heavens, Gwyn, how unspeakably unfortunate!"

Knowing her mother, Gwyneth didn't suppose that she was the slightest bit exercised on behalf of the young cousin. She merely thought it dreadfully unfortunate that Gwyneth's own past should rear up beside her, threatening her present wonderful security.

"What did you do?"

"I went, first of all, to see Terry. I tried to make him see that he must leave Paula alone—Paula was the girl, of course."

Mrs. Vilner gave a slight exclamation of despair that Gwyneth should have allowed herself to be so hopelessly sidetracked.

"He wouldn't hear of it—said he really held all the trump cards himself——"

"Which was true, of course," interrupted Mrs. Vilner sharply.

Gwyneth shrugged.

"In a way, yes. He could ruin me. But then I could also ruin him, possibly put him within measurable distance of prison."

"Nonsense. That sort of man knows how to get away every time. I hope you weren't such a fool as to threaten."

"I suppose I did. I felt I must do anything to save Paula from what had happened to me."

"Good heavens, child, couldn't you leave the girl to look after herself?"

"Why?" Gwyneth's voice was extremely cold. "What sort of beast should I have been if—knowing what I did— I made no attempt to rescue her?"

"But if you scared him away, he was almost bound to take his revenge by exposing you."

Gwyneth was silent. She supposed that was all too true.

"Well, anyway, he refused to go," she said slowly at last. "Apparently his—his real wife had died some time during the last few years. He likes Paula—he isn't capable of loving, of course, but I think he genuinely likes her—and she will inherit a great deal of money. Actually, he would probably never do anything better for himself *than* marry her."

"Then"—Mrs. Vilner's expression became one of cool satisfaction—"then you mean that silence is just as important to him as to you?"

"Exactly."

"Oh, Gwyneth! And you had the sense to come to some arrangement about it—to keep quiet, too?"

"I came to no arrangement at all," Gwyneth retorted sharply. "I couldn't let Paula go into that with her eyes entirely closed. I tried to make her understand something of what he was really like—explained that he had already treated me foully. I—I didn't tell her everything—about Toby, for instance. I made out that it was a case of— seduction." She closed her lips tightly on the hateful word.

Mrs. Vilner went quite pale, not because the word appalled her, but because she could scarcely bear to think that Gwyneth had tried to throw her safety away, as she considered.

"Gwyneth, I sometimes think you don't deserve to escape danger," she exclaimed bitterly. "Can you never let well alone?"

"It wasn't "well", Mother," Gwyneth said dryly. "It was remarkably "ill". But, anyway"—she frowned and sighed impatiently—"Paula refused to believe me."

"She——" Mrs. Vilner looked at her daughter in stupefaction. "Really, child, your father would say a special Providence looked after you, in spite of everything. It is as though even your own folly can't ruin you. Thank heaven this other girl seems to be even more stupid than you."

Gwyneth made a little grimace at this candour.

"I don't know about that. But, anyway, Terry had got there first with Paula—told her some convincing story about my having fallen badly for him in my youth, and never having forgiven him for not returning my affection. He had even told her to be prepared for some fantastic story from me—that I would stick at nothing in my jealous fury. I might as well have talked to the wind. Nothing short of Toby's birth certificate would have convinced her——"

"And even that wouldn't," was Mrs. Vilner's cynical amendment. "The father is given as "unknown". I took care of that."

Gwyneth winced slightly, but she made no comment.

"So that, as things are"—Mrs. Vilner was positively cheerful again—"Terry will probably marry this girl and remain silent because it suits him as well as you?"

"It's at least possible. It's a beastly position, but I don't see that there is anything else I can do."

"Of course there isn't! Even now the position is anything but secure, but the most powerful guarantee you can have is that this man's own interests happen to run in line with yours. Does he know about the child, as well as everything else?" she added sharply.

"He guessed as soon as he saw Toby," Gwyneth said shortly.

"And it made no difference?"

"What sort of difference do you suppose it would make?"

"Oh, I was only thinking that the hardest and most contemptible of men can sometimes wallow in sentiment over any reproduction of themselves. It's an odd thing, parenthood."

"Yes," Gwyneth said slowly, "it is. But I don't think you need worry about Terry being violently attached to Toby. I should say he has no feeling about him at all."

"Splendid," Mrs. Vilner said heartily, as Toby's voice sounded in the hall.

He came running in a moment later, full of interest as usual because there was a visitor. He kissed Gwyneth and went at once to Mrs. Vilner.

"Hello. Are you my granny?" he asked.

It was not the happiest form of introduction, and Gwyneth bit her lip, but Toby immediately and innocently retrieved the position by leaning against Mrs. Vilner and saying:

"You're not at all *old*, are you?"

"A great deal older than you are," Mrs. Vilner said, patting his cheek. "What makes you think I'm your grandmother?"

"Betty said my granny was coming to tea."

"I see. Does he call you Mother and Father, Gwyneth?"

Gwyneth nodded, while Toby said:

"I call her Mummy. She *is* my mummy."

Gwyneth bit her lip again and Mrs. Vilner smiled dryly.

"And my daddy is at the office. He has to work very hard."

"Does he?"

Toby nodded. "Yes, he does. To make lots of money," he added informatively.

"So that you can spend it?"

Toby looked rather serious at that, and slowly dragged two pennies from the pocket of his small trousers.

He was still regarding them when Van came in a moment or two later, and Gwyneth called him to come to tea.

Van greeted his mother-in-law quite agreeably. They neither liked nor disliked each other, and their relations were always completely on the surface. As he bent to kiss Gwyneth and to ruffle Toby's hair, Toby pushed his two pennies under Van's notice.

"Did you have to work very hard for these?" he asked, his voice even more than usually gruff with anxiety.

"Um? What's that?" Van examined the pennies. "I don't think so. Are they special pennies?"

"They're my pennies," Toby explained.

Van smiled slightly, still rather puzzled.

"Why should I have to work hard for these?"

"My granny," stated Toby firmly, "said you had to work hard to make money for me to spend."

"I see." Van took the pennies thoughtfully in his rather long fingers. "Well, what can we do about it?"

Toby put his hands behind him, though his eyes remained longingly on the pennies.

"I don't want them," he said with palpable inaccuracy.

"Don't you?"

Toby shook his head.

"Because I have to work for them?"

Toby nodded.

With a sudden laugh, Van caught him up and hugged him.

"You little 'goose! You don't make any difference. I don't have to work any harder because I have you. I shouldn't mind if I had to," he added with a quick kiss on Toby's cheek.

"Why, Van, how fond you are of that child," Mrs. Vilner exclaimed with a surprised laugh, and Van flushed slightly.

"Of course," he said shortly, and held Toby for a moment longer.

"Toby is strangely like me when he looks at Van in that way," thought Gwyneth suddenly, as she watched this scene without comment. The child looked extremely fair with his face very near Van's dark cheek, and his wide blue eyes were very like his mother's, as he slowly took back his pennies. It was true—he did look at Van with the same air of loving gratitude that her eyes expressed when she thanked him for being good to her.

"Well—now tea." Van seemed a little impatient of this scene, now he came to think about it, and he changed the subject at once. "Paula came in to see me in the office today—though she knows she is not supposed to," he added in parenthesis. "However, that makes no difference to her, of course, especially when she has what she considers good news. I hardly think it will please you, though, Gwyn," he added with a smile.

"No? What is it?"

"She's going to marry her Terry. The whole thing has got as far as a handsome engagement ring, and I understand they won't be wasting very much time on a long engagement. The idea is to be married fairly early in the New Year.

Gwyneth paled slightly and bit her lip.

"Do her parents approve?"

"Oh, apparently, quite heartily. I don't think he's got very much money, but then, of course, Paula will have a great deal."

"And they have no objection to her husband living on her?"

Van shrugged.

"I expect it will be arranged a little more tactfully than that, Gwyn."

"It's the same thing, whatever you call it." The contempt and bitterness in her voice made her husband raise his eyebrows.

"You're really rather hard on him." Then he turned to Mrs. Vilner, whose expression of mild interest would not have disgraced a professional actress. "Paula is a young cousin of mine, and Gwyneth doesn't at all like the man who has been running after her."

"Well, well, why bother?" Mrs. Vilner said comfortingly. "No doubt the girl knows her own mind best. Actually, Gwyneth dear, it isn't your business, is it?"

Gwyneth looked at her mother, and pushed back her hair with a troubled little gesture.

"No," she said slowly, "I suppose you're right. If it has got as far as an engagement, it really isn't my business."

The subject of Paula and Terry was not mentioned again, but later, when Van was working in his study, and Gwyneth had already gone to bed, Mrs. Vilner came to her bedroom door.

"May I come in, Gwyneth?"

"Yes." Gwyneth was oddly reminded of her mother coming to deliver a few words of trenchant advice a night or two before her wedding.

Advice was pleasantly mixed with congratulation this time, however.

"There, you see, Gwyneth, it has all worked out splendidly," she said without any preamble. "He stands to lose at least as much as you if he talks. It's quite wonderful that you should have such a safeguard."

"Quite wonderful," Gwyneth agreed a trifle dryly. "But I must say I wish Paula had a few safeguards, too."

"Oh, she'll do very well," Mrs. Vilner declared, with a fine disregard for anything which happened outside her own immediate circle. "And I must congratulate you on your management of *l'affaire* Toby, too. Van is as docile as can be. You have trained him wonderfully."

"Van loves Toby," Gwyneth said coldly. "That's all there is to it."

"Oh, no doubt." Her mother spoke almost absently, and her daughter looked at her curiously.

"You haven't the faintest feeling about him, have you?" she said.

"Who?—Van? I'm really most attached to him," Mrs. Vilner exclaimed.

"No, I didn't mean Van. I meant Toby."

"Why should I have any overwhelming feeling about him? I hardly know the child. Quite a dear little fellow, of course."

"Mother, he's your grandchild," Gwyneth said slowly. "Your only grandchild. Doesn't that make any difference?"

Mrs. Vilner shrugged very slightly.

"In the circumstances, I had almost overlooked the fact," she admitted quite coolly. "Naturally, I haven't any of the usual feeling about him. No doubt I shall get fond of him in time."

"No doubt," Gwyneth agreed dryly as she bade her mother good night. But she watched her go, with the faintest smile of protest. Her mother would never grow fond of Toby, because she would never grow fond of anyone.

It didn't matter, of course, because darling Toby didn't really need her. He had his mother now—and he had Van. Van, who was so good to him and so fond of him. Sometimes he looked at Toby as he might have looked at a son of his own. Or was that just a happy fancy?

Anyway, as Gwyneth put up her hand to switch out the light, she gave a quick sigh of content. Without looking at things quite as Mother did, one could dare to hope that the problem of Toby and the problem of Paula had rather settled themselves.

CHAPTER NINE

MRS. VILNER stayed only a couple of days with her daughter after that. She had found out all that she had come to find out, and, so far as she could see, the situation was satisfactory.

At least, considering all the very dangerous elements which went to its make-up, the situation was satisfactory.

"Now remember, Gwyneth," she said, as she bade her daughter good-bye, "you really owe it to Van and the child, too, to keep silent. Don't have any more quixotic ideas about saving unintelligent young women from the results of their own folly. This Paula seems to be quite blessedly dense. She simply doesn't want you to cut your throat on her behalf. In any case, of course, she is as likely as not to be happy with this man. Quite a lot of women would far rather have a bounder than no man at all. She may be that kind of woman."

"You needn't worry," Gwyneth said. "If I think Paula is likely to be reasonably happy with Terry—and it does seem more than likely—I certainly shouldn't interfere for the sake of interfering."

"Very sensible," her mother approved. And she took her way back to her home in the country, fairly sure that, for the moment at least, her daughter could be relied on to do what she herself called 'the sensible thing'.

That afternoon, Paula came to see Gwyneth.

She was looking extremely happy, and prettier than ever.

"Oh, Gwyn dear, I have so wanted to see you! Because after I had called in to see Van and had told *him* instead of *you*, I thought how cowardly and silly it seemed, and I wondered if you were offended."

"Not in the least." Gwyneth laughed as she returned Paula's kiss. "I'm really very glad indeed if you think you're going to be happy with Terry."

"Why, of *course* I am. It's the best and loveliest thing

145

that ever happened to me, and, thank heaven, the parents haven't been too sticky!"

"Have they been "sticky" at all?"

"Well"—Paula made a little face—"Terry really hasn't got much money, you know." (Gwyneth just bit back a dry "No, he never had.") "But, as Daddy very sensibly said in the end, one hardly expects artists to, somehow. And of course, I have quite a disgusting lot myself, and it's stupid to let *that* stand in the way, isn't it? I mean, the money's *there,* so why shouldn't we be happy on it, without bothering about which of us it belongs to?"

"Very altruistic," Gwyneth commented with a smile, but she was secretly thinking that it might not be at all a bad thing to have Terry financially dependent on his wife. At least, that would be a sharp inducement for him to behave himself.

"Gwyneth, you—you don't feel awful about it any more, do you?" Paula was looking at her very anxiously.

"No. I never did feel "awful", in the sense you mean ——" Gwyneth broke off a little embarrassedly. It was rather difficult to see how to make the changeover. But she tried again. "It would be silly to pretend that I think well of Terry, because I don't, but perhaps I never saw anything but the bad side of him——"

"That was it, of course," Paula interrupted eagerly. "I know he *has* faults, of course, but then who hasn't?"

Gwyneth suppressed the reply she would like to have made to this comfortable platitude, and patted Paula's arm.

"Anyway, Paula dear, if you're happy and your parents approve, and Terry looks like making you"—she swallowed slightly—"a good husband, it certainly isn't my business to try to make trouble."

"Oh, Gwyn! I'm so glad you feel like that. I really thought you would, in the end, but I was quite miserable at the idea that you might be feeling unhappy because—because—you know what."

Gwyneth saw she was still under the misapprehension that, once having loved Terry, one could scarcely do anything but go on loving him.

"Don't think about that any more. If you want me to put it into words, I adore my own husband, and there isn't another man in the world so far as I'm concerned."

146

"Really? I can't imagine anyone feeling like that about Van. Still, he's very nice. Love's a queer thing," she added profoundly.

And Gwyneth thought that indeed it was, if it made Paula find Terry perfect while she couldn't understand what anyone saw in Van.

"You know, really my people are rather old sports when it comes to the point," Paula remarked after a short pause.

"Yes?" Gwyneth smiled inquiringly. "You mean because they are letting you do what you want?"

"Oh no—at least, not only that. But my father was frightfully understanding in the end about it being a rather rotten position for Terry if he had to—well, to feel that all the money was mine."

"Oh?" Gwyneth's exclamation this time was faintly alarmed as well as questioning. "What did he do in order to—spare Terry's feelings?"

"He's actually settling quite a large sum of money on him."

"Paula, he's not!" Not for the first time, Gwyneth reflected for an incredulous moment on the extreme gullibility of strict people—once they decide to relax.

"Yes, he is. As a matter of fact, you know, it's very sensible as well as sweet of him. He would leave Terry quite a bit, in the ordinary way, and this gets round death duties and that sort of thing quite satisfactorily."

"But, Paula, why not settle it on *you?*"

"Oh, I inherited quite a lot from my grandparents. There's a good deal of money in our family, one way and another," she added carelessly, and Gwyneth wondered if she had made that very attractive statement to Terry, too. If so, it was no wonder he identified himself so closely with them! "It would be ridiculous," Paula went on in a reasonable tone, "if, just for the sort of greedy principle of the thing, I hung on to everything and poor Terry was just a rich woman's husband."

Gwyneth was silent, thinking how wonderfully 'poor Terry' had fallen on his feet, and how extremely little hold Paula was going to have over him, after all.

"You don't approve, do you?" Paula asked with a smile.

"No, Paula, if you want my opinion, I don't."

"Well, *I'm* awfully happy about it. It makes things so

much simpler and nicer. And, as you said yourself, if we're happy about things, that's the really important point, isn't it?"

That hadn't been quite what Gwyneth had said, of course, but she let it pass. Perhaps her fears and imaginings were something of an impertinence now that everything was so definitely settled. Certainly no one would be interested in them. The best thing was to keep them to herself.

But later, to Van, she did say:

"Don't you think it's very unwise? Paula's father is apparently going to settle quite a large sum of money on Terry."

"Very unwise," Van agreed lazily. "Hang on to your own money until it leaves you of its own accord, is my theory. It does that soon enough, in any case."

"No, Van—really, I'm serious."

"Are you, darling? Well then, what is the idea in feathering Muirkirk's nest for him? Hasn't he anything to feather it with himself?"

"No. I suppose that's the truth of the matter."

"Why on earth Paula wants to marry a man who can't even afford to keep her, I don't know," Van declared with an impatient little shrug. "But it's always the way with these rich only daughters. Find some fellow who has loads of charm and a big overdraft and keep him in clover for the rest of his life. That seems to be the great idea. I don't think Muirkirk is quite the villain you do, but I'm hanged if I've much respect for him. Before I'd live on my wife I'd black shoes."

"I should have thought Paula's father would have argued on those lines, too," Gwyneth said.

"Perhaps he did, poor fellow. Paula has a quick way of dealing with any opposition she meets. Besides, of course, in spite of everything she says, they are really very indulgent towards her, when it comes to the point. It's the usual situation of rather elderly parents with an only—and attractive daughter. They keep a close eye on her, to begin with, then when they capitulate, they do the thing handsomely. Probably they're telling themselves now that all they really want is dear Paula's happiness, and this is the way to give it to her."

148

Gwyneth sighed.

"I suppose that is it."

"She seems very happy, doesn't she?"

"Oh, very."

"Then I shouldn't worry. Some women enjoy squandering money on a man. You can't teach them wisdom and they probably will never learn of their own accord. Anyway, perhaps they get their money's worth out of the pleasure of doing it."

"Paula isn't as silly as that, though."

"Not quite—but very nearly," was Van's verdict. And at that, they left the subject.

Even if Terry were going to acquire a small fortune, as well as a wife, in the New Year, there was really nothing to be done about it.

For Gwyneth and Van, the first Christmas in their own home passed happily. The vague invitation to spend it with Gwyneth's parents did not materialize—Gwyneth had not supposed it would—and they preferred, in any case, to have it alone together, making it Toby's first real home festivity. The child was excited and pleased over every detail, and his delight was sweeter to Gwyneth—and indeed to Van—than any present of their own.

He was used to a Christmas tree—they had always had a big one at Greystones—but the personal stocking and the home celebrations which naturally centred round him were quite outside his previous experience. He told Gwyneth afterwards that it was "the very best Christmas there'd ever been."

She thought it unlikely that he could remember more than, perhaps, three with which to compare it, but she laughed and was pleased with the compliment to their efforts, all the same.

That year January was fine and bright, and almost every afternoon she and Toby used to go into the Park. He had several little friends there now, in addition to the greatly envied owner of the puppy, and it was even warm enough sometimes for Gwyneth to sit down on a bench in the pale, wintry sunshine for a short while and watch her little boy tearing about happily with the others.

She used to think then how happy she was and how very greatly blessed. She had in Van the best and dearest of husbands, and Toby, who had once seemed irrevocably lost to her, was living with her now as the treasured little son that he was.

It was true that the last seal of security had still not been set on her happiness, but at least everything had been made as safe as one could possibly hope. And if sometimes nervous anxiety overwhelmed her and made her wonder in panic again what would happen if Van ever found out, she reminded herself immediately that no one could expect perfect happiness. She must be grateful—and more than grateful—for what she had.

One afternoon Gwyneth was out with Toby, and he had begged her to sit down for a while and watch him play.

"It's most important," he explained earnestly, his woolly-gloved hands planted on her knee in a characteristic manner. "We're all going to race and you must say which is first and second and third. I've told them you'll know because you know everything."

"Very well," Gwyneth said, accepting the heavy responsibility of so much knowledge.

So she sat there for some time, acting as umpire for several panting little boys and one skinny little girl who, most disconcertingly, contrived to beat them all every time.

After a while they grew rather tired of this and began some other game in which her services were not required. Relieved from her duties, Gwyneth glanced round idly. She wondered whether she should walk briskly to the main gate and back, for it was getting a trifle chilly, but she felt lazy, too, and could not quite make up her mind to move.

There was no one else about except a few strollers. Then, walking slowly and deep in conversation, two other people came into view. She watched them without interest for a few seconds—until she realized with a disagreeable shock that the man was Terry.

The woman with him should have been Paula, of course, but she certainly was not. Someone much older— oddly familiar, and yet not really well known to Gwyneth.

They were almost abreast of her now, still too deep in conversation to have noticed her. And then, with a start that made her feel physically sick, Gwyneth recognized her. It was the woman who had come and fetched Terry

150

from the hotel, all those years ago. The wife—who was supposed to be dead.

Whether her start attracted his attention or whether he just happened to glance her way Gwyneth could not have said, but at almost the same moment as she recognized the woman, Terry looked at her.

Her own expression must have told him something, and if she had been in any doubt before, the flash of angry dismay in his eyes would have told her that her guess was correct. A second or two too late, she tried to make her face blank of all surprise and horror, but she was afraid he had seen all that was necessary already.

With the faintest sign of recognition from him and none at all from the woman, they passed on—and Gwyneth was left, agitated and trembling, wondering what on earth she was to do with this horrible piece of knowledge which had come her way.

So Terry was still married! His wife was not dead at all. This marriage he was going to palm off on Paula was no more real than the one with Gwyneth herself. It was a more complicated and much more profitable fraud—that was all.

And Paula's father was to settle a large sum of money on him—make him comfortable for life! Then, when he had had enough of Paula, he would decamp, taking his newfound capital with him. Very simply—very effective. The woman was no doubt in it, too, or if not, she would be paid well (with Paula's money) to keep out of the way for a while.

It was probably quite outside Terry's intentions that she should have been here even now. Perhaps she had turned difficult—he had had to persuade her—discuss with her the amount of the bribe. Oh, he was the most vile——

A shadow fell across her, and, looking up, Gwyneth saw that Terry was standing beside her—alone, looking down at her with a mixture of doubt and bravado.

"Well, Gwyneth," he dropped down on the seat beside her, "it's quite an unexpected pleasure to see you here."

"I often come with my little boy. He likes to play here," she said coldly.

Should she make another attempt to hide her knowledge?—keep it to herself and try to put him off his guard

151

until she could decide what she was going to do? It might be best.

Terry was looking away thoughtfully now to where Toby was deep in consultation with his friends.

"He is a very charming child—our son." The thin, steely note of danger was meant as a threat, she knew—a warning that he really had her completely in his power. Then there was little doubt he knew that *she* knew. It was scarcely worthwhile going through the farce of pretending. And yet one must. In any case, she would not let that statement go unchallenged.

"I don't know why you speak so absurdly about Toby," she said coolly and proudly. "It's an extremely dangerous thing to say and quite without foundation, incidentally?"

"Dangerous for me or for you, Gwyneth?"

"For you. There *is* a law of libel which touches even such scoundrels as you, I suppose."

"But such a very dangerous one to invoke, don't you think?"

She was silent, and after a moment he took the initiative about the other question and remarked:

"You know why I came back to speak to you, of course?"

"I'm afraid I don't. I should have thought it would be much more comfortable for both of us if you made no attempt to speak to me except when the presence of other people forced it on us."

She did that so well that, at first, she saw he almost believed her. Then Toby came running up to ask her something very important. He stopped in surprise on seeing Terry, and said rather doubtfully: "Hello."

"Hello. Don't you remember me?"

"No," Toby said, but it was rather obvious that he did, and Gwyneth realized that, for some reason, he didn't like Terry.

"We ought to go home now, darling," she said as naturally as possible to Toby.

"Oh, Mummy, just *five* minutes more!" he begged.

"I think——"

"Suppose you let him have five minutes," Terry's voice suggested smoothly: "It might be a good idea."

She bit her lip furiously, feeling the tug of the chain and longing to resist.

Toby looked at her hopefully, and after a moment she spoke with a curtness that was not meant for the child.

"All right. Five minutes only."

Toby galloped off, and Terry laughed quietly.

"So you aren't very good at recognizing people?" he murmured, but she only said:

"I don't know what you're talking about."

"Come, Gwyneth. I'll use the words you once used to me—I don't know that it's any good hedging. Of course you recognized her. Your expression gave you away."

She didn't say anything, and he added almost carelessly:

"Well, what are you going to do about it?"

"I don't know," Gwyneth said slowly, and that, of course, was the literal truth.

"May I suggest that it would be much wiser to do nothing?"

She looked at him with fear and dislike.

"Do you really expect me to do nothing?"

"I expect you to make a great many protests to begin with, and then to decide—very wisely—that it isn't your business."

"I suppose when you have got all you can out of Paula and her family, you will desert her?"

"You haven't a very high opinion of me, have you?" he remarked with a smile.

"No. Why should I? I know you too well."

He paid that the tribute of an amused grimace.

"Well, whether you believe me or not—I really do intend to settle down with Paula——"

"I *don't* believe you," she stated baldly.

"—And I'm not expecting to have any trouble from— the lady you saw just now."

"You mean you're paying her with Paula's money to keep out of the way?"

He shrugged.

"I don't believe that, either," Gwyneth told him shortly. "Why don't you get a divorce if you really no longer have any interest in each other, and don't intend to see each other again?"

"My dear, do you really think I could afford to appear

153

in a court of law?—even in connection with anything so simple as a divorce suit," he said with shameless simplicity.

There was something in that, she supposed.

"Anyway, that is beside the point," she said impatiently. "The fact is that Paula won't be really married to you—whether you stay with her or whether you choose to desert her later."

"There is so much in the way one looks at these things, Gwyneth. If *you* don't tell her, she'll think she really is my wife. That's quite sufficient for her happiness, you know."

"Until you choose to leave her."

"But I've told you—I'm staying with her."

"We're arguing in a circle." Gwyneth rose to her feet with an air of finality. "Don't ask me what I'm going to do. I don't know. But—oh, why don't you go away again, Terry? Why don't you go?—instead of hanging around waiting to prey on silly young women because there happens to be money in it!"

"Don't be absurd, my dear. What man in his senses would turn his back on a charming wife and financial security for life?"

She called to Toby without answering that, and he came running across the grass to her.

"So you don't know what you're going to do?" There was an angry little sneer in Terry's voice.

"No."

"Very well. But don't imagine I shall be in any similar state of indecision if you do give me away. I shall know exactly what *I* am going to do."

And with that final threat, he turned away and left her, striding along the path with an air of purpose, his footsteps ringing sharply on the half frozen ground.

"Mummy, are we going home now?"

Toby's voice roused her from her thoughts and recalled her to the fact that she was standing staring after Terry in her perplexity.

She glanced down then at the little boy.

"Yes, Toby."

As they turned away he thrust his hand into hers and remarked:

"It was a lovely afternoon, wasn't it?"

And what could she say but "Yes" again?

During all the rest of that day she tried to come to some sort of decision. On the face of it, it was criminal to let Paula—and her parents, too—be exploited by Terry. His assurance that he would stick by Paula was scarcely worth the breath behind it. And, in any case, what sort of a position was that for a decent young-girl?

And yet, if she were personally responsible for giving Terry away, she could hardly expect much mercy from him. It had not required his last words to let her know that.

The next morning came, still without her having arrived at any decision, and with the morning's post came a letter from Paula's mother. For a wild moment Gwyneth hoped that they had found out something for themselves and were writing for some sort of advice about how to deal with detaching Paula from Terry. But the fantastic hope faded as she read the formal lines. It was simply that she wanted Van and Gwyneth to come to dinner the following week, and it seemed that 'Paula's fiancé' would be there.

"We'll have to go, of course," Van said with a slight touch of resignation.

"Do you mind?"

"Not more than I mind other stuffy rather boring evenings. And they are kindly people who mean well."

'Stuffy' perhaps—but 'boring'—certainly not, thought Gwyneth. She only wished it could be. That would be infinitely preferable to the uncomfortably dramatic affair she was afraid it was going to be.

But if she chose to give Terry away before then, of course, the dinner party would not take place at all.

Oh, if only something would happen so that the onus of taking action was not on her! Why hadn't *Paula* seen that woman with Terry, instead of herself? Why hadn't her parents been suspicious—loath to part with a penny of their money—or one of a dozen other things which might have put Terry off?

Why did *she* have to be responsible for deciding on the right thing, regardless of how it wrecked everything for herself?

"It's too cruel," Gwyneth thought distractedly. "It would be bad enough if someone else did it to me—but that I should have to put the match to the gunpowder myself is too awful."

It was no wonder she hesitated from day to day, telling herself that there was no desperate need for urgency until every other chance of the marriage failing had had time to operate.

Suppose, by some miracle, Paula grew tired of him, found out for herself what kind of man he was, was completely put off by something he did? Or suppose he discovered an even better proposition than Paula?

She knew it was illogical and absurd to go over these more than remote possibilities. It was like saying to oneself: "Suppose I won the Pools?" But just as that is sometimes a spurious consolation for an empty purse, so these fantastic improbabilities seemed a weak sort of inspiration of hope.

On the night of the dinner party Gwyneth dressed with particular care. She wanted to make herself look self-possessed and sophisticated, so that Terry might not feel so completely sure of his power.

But Van's comment was not encouraging in that respect. He smiled at her and said: "Darling, how adorably and absurdly young you look tonight."

"What! In black, and with ear-rings?"

"I don't know what it is," he said with masculine vagueness. "Except—yes, the black dress makes your skin look almost childishly fair."

"And the ear-rings? Don't even they save me?"

But he laughed and took her face between his hands.

"The ear-rings, sweetheart, are just a lovely sort of joke."

They were nothing of the sort, of course, but she liked it when he said such things, all the same.

Just before they left the flat she went into Toby's room to see that he was all right. To her surprise, he was awake, but lying there quite contentedly.

He smiled at her—sleepily but with beaming affection —as she bent over him to kiss him.

"I like those funny things in your ears," he said. "They flap, like elephant ears."

The compliment might not be very happily expressed, but the tone was unmistakably admiring, and Gwyneth laughed.

She hugged him and he immediately put his arms up round her neck and hugged her in return.

Impossible—impossible! she thought, that he was Terry's son. The child of a good-for-nothing, cruel swindler. He was so much more the sort of son that Van might have—

And at that she suddenly found the tears very near, because he was not Van's, and Van wouldn't even want him in the house if he knew the truth.

"Go to sleep, darling, and pleasant dreams." She patted his cheek and he immediately snuggled down again under the bed-clothes.

"Pleasant party," he said politely, and she went out of the room, laughing a little.

But when she was outside the door she didn't laugh any more.

Pleasant party! No, it was hardly likely to be that.

Van was waiting for her, and they went out to the car together.

"Sanderton rang up from the office a few minutes ago," he said as they drove away from the flat. "He's staying on there tonight until ten or eleven because we are expecting a very important cable from America late this evening. It's just possible that I might have to go along, too, later. He'll phone me at Norbury if necessary——"

"You mean you might have to leave me there?" Gwyneth sounded slightly startled in spite of all her efforts to hide the fact.

"Yes. You don't mind, do you?"

She didn't answer at once, and he said:

"They aren't at all alarming people, you know. Formal but perfectly friendly. Besides, it isn't like you to need social support." He seemed surprised and a little amused.

"No, no, of course not. It's all right," she amended.

"Sure?"

"Quite sure."

He glanced at her, she knew, not entirely convinced. But evidently he decided to take her answer at its face value, and nothing more was said.

They were silent after that. They often were when they went out driving together, but it was the silence of perfect companionship. No doubt he was pursuing the train of thought in connection with his business affairs, she told herself. She was free to reflect on the disagreeable possibility of having to face whatever crisis there was tonight, alone. Or, if there were no crisis—then she might be forced to allow Terry to take her home by taxi.

It was difficult to say which thought was more unpleasant, and she was looking unusually grave when they arrived at Paula's home.

Actually, Gwyneth found, on arrival, the house at Norbury was nothing like so forbidding as Paula and Van had suggested. Large and not very modern, yet it had an air of rich-toned comfort which suggested a very pleasant sufficiency of this world's goods.

Throughout the house there reigned a rich, carpeted silence which it was difficult to associate with Paula. But then Paula's parents were also a little difficult to associate with her, Gwyneth found, when she and Van entered the long drawing-room and were greeted by them.

Mrs. Stacey, tall and heavily dignified, wore a dress of heavy amethyst silk, which had probably cost more than anything Gwyneth had ever worn in her life, though she reckoned to spend a good deal on her clothes.

Mr. Stacey was rosy-cheeked and bushy-haired—an unexpectedly cheerful little man, and nothing like so dignified as his wife. They were both at least sixty, Gwyneth saw, and indeed Mr. Stacey, at least, was probably not far off seventy.

Apparently Van enjoyed their almost unlimited approval, and it seemed probable that she was to be allowed to share this.

"We were sorry, indeed, not to be able to attend your wedding in the summer," Mrs. Stacey told her, "but, of course, my husband and I do very little travelling nowadays, and it seemed too much of an undertaking to come quite so far."

Gwyneth assured her hostess that she quite understood —though she secretly felt convinced that old Mr. Stacey, if left to his own choice, would certainly have undertaken an even longer journey. He seemed game for a good many more things than his wife, but was rather firmly suppressed if he showed signs of breaking out in any unorthodox direction. It was from him, undoubtedly, that Paula inherited her more headstrong qualities, and, in consequence,

Gwyneth thought, it was probably he, rather than the mother, who had capitulated so completely to Terry's onslaught.

Conversation took a very correct and conventional turn. They talked of the mildness of the weather, their pleasure in Paula's engagement, the possibility of a foreign honeymoon for her, while Gwyneth thought:

"How awful! They're so completely and utterly taken in, and they're the kind to blame themselves terribly afterwards if anything happened to their darling. I can't let it go on." And yet to speak meant—what?

"Mr. Muirkirk," announced the au pair girl, and Terry breezed into the room.

Until then, Gwyneth had felt that he could not do anything but strike a slightly incongruous note—in these surroundings, with which he had nothing in common. But she was quite mistaken. Nothing could have been more complete than Terry's assumption of the attributes and qualities most suited to the Stacey's expectation of what a son-in-law should be.

He bent over Mrs. Stacey's hand, and then respectfully kissed the large, smooth cheek offered. Royalty saluting royalty could not have done it better. He called Mr. Stacey 'sir', and deferred to him in most things, listening with pleasant attention to almost every word he uttered. And, while Paula showed a faint impatience at the slow tempo of the household, he accommodated himself to it with magnificent good humour tinged with respect.

It was not lost on Van, Gwyneth saw, and while she felt nothing but indignation and contempt for what she knew was the exploiting of these decent people, he was evidently very genuinely amused by what he believed to be a piece of harmless and tactful diplomacy.

Terry greeted her with charming courtesy, and Van with more than friendliness. His effrontery was so staggering that Gwyneth was frightened. It was as though he knew he was invincible, and scarcely bothered to suppose that anyone could think him anything else.

Presently they moved into the slightly gloomy dining-room, where heavy mahogany furniture and a deep-piled maroon-coloured carpet seemed to suggest that here eating took place as a very solemn rite.

Tall, steadily-burning candles shed pools of light on the highly-polished table, and the very exquisite lace table-mats seemed to float on the surface of a dark pool. The flower decorations were conventional but lavish, and they had evidently been chosen quite regardless of expense.

Each course of the meal was perfectly served, perfectly cooked, and, to tell the truth, perfectly chosen. Mrs. Stacey might not believe in 'patronizing gay restaurants', but she certainly knew how to provide a meal which defied criticism, in her own house.

Gwyneth's intelligence paid tribute to it, while her sense of enjoyment was left untouched. It was impossible to enjoy the most perfect of food when one's thoughts were in a turmoil and one's confidence in open revolt against one's fondest wishes.

"We were just talking about your plans for a foreign honeymoon," Van remarked to Terry across the table.

"Oh yes?" Terry exchanged a smile with Paula. "I should actually have liked a tour round the world myself, but we decided it would mean too great a change for Mr. and Mrs. Stacey. One doesn't expect to have one's only daughter taken away quite so completely and abruptly." This time the smile was directed upon Mrs. Stacey, whose slight inclination of the head was evidently meant to convey that she appreciated Terry's thought for them.

Gwyneth watched in silent but incredulous astonishment. It would have been impossible for a casual observer to suppose that any but Terry's money would have paid for the suggested world tour. No—the change of plans was due solely to his exquisite consideration for others, and not at all to the fact that he was drawing lavishly on his fiancée's family for his future support.

"You chose Switzerland, didn't you?" Terry was addressing himself to her, she found, and the conversation was apparently still circling round the topic of honeymoons.

"Yes. We only managed to snatch ten days, but we had a wonderful time." She was surprised, herself, at the agreeable cordiality with which she managed to produce that.

"Ah, that's the worst of you business magnates," Terry turned to Van again. "Business must come first, even on a honeymoon. Now, we good-for-nothing artists can laze

160

away a month or two, and all anyone says is "disgusting how that fellow neglects his work, but then what do you expect from an artist?" And he laughed so pleasantly at the joke against himself that everyone joined in, just to show how absurd was the disparaging reference.

"But then you work very hard when you *are* at it," Paula protested.

Terry shrugged and smiled.

"You've only seen me working on something I specially enjoy," he told her. And then Gwyneth was not at all surprised to learn that he was busying himself on a portrait of Mrs. Stacey.

"It's really wonderful," she thought, with something like reluctant admiration for his sheer rascality. "He had the sense to choose her rather than the old man. She was the difficult part of the problem, as I thought. He can manage his future father-in-law with one hand.

"Terry is *extremely* gifted," Mrs. Stacey said to Van, and Gwyneth thought that was certainly true, though not in quite the way she meant.

"We're having a marvellous studio built, all along one side of the house," Paula explained. "Two stories high and lots of the right sort of light—I never know which it is. Anyway, Terry is delighted with it."

The whole Stacey family appeared to share Terry's delight, Gwyneth noticed at that moment.

"A very bad arrangement," Van told Paula rather teasingly. "You shouldn't have your husband working at home. You'll be dreadfully sick of him before the first year's out."

"Oh *no!* It's much more fun than saying good-bye immediately after breakfast and wondering after that if he'll even be in to tea. I think Gwyneth's an angel to put up so well with all those hours alone."

"Gwyneth is quite an exceptional person in every way," Van asserted, still with an air of banter, but this time with an under-current of meaning.

Gwyneth smiled.

"I don't mind my own company," she said, "and in any case, I'm not alone."

"Oh no. Of course, there's Toby now, isn't there? And I hear you really are adopting him permanently, as you wanted. But a little boy isn't really very much company, is he?"

"Toby is." Gwyneth was quite firm about that, while Mrs. Stacey remarked judicially:

"An intelligent child can be *quite* a little companion. At six, Paula, you certainly were."

"Oh, I don't expect I was a tenth as quaint and amusing as Toby," Paula declared generously. "He's quite adorable."

"My daughter tells me he is a most attractive child," Mrs. Stacey said graciously to Gwyneth. "So fortunate, because, of course, it is a terrible risk."

"Adopting a child, you mean?"

"Yes."

"We didn't feel there was much risk about it," Van put in, with that casual firmness that always made Gwyneth feel the whole thing was so reasonable and justifiable—not simply a wild and emotional impulse, as it must seem to some people.

"I think the most remarkable thing is their objective view of it," Terry declared to Mrs. Stacey. "I don't believe they even insisted on knowing anything of the child's antecedents."

"Do you think that was very wise?" Mrs. Stacey's tone expressed perfectly that *she* did not.

"But there weren't any known, in any case, were there?" Paula said.

"There must have been some sort of record at the orphanage, unless he was actually a foundling," her mother insisted.

"I don't think he was that," Van said. "But Gwyn and I both felt that the less we knew about his previous circumstances, the more he would seem like our own."

Mrs. Stacey sucked her under-lip thoughtfully and shook her head.

"But the parents might have been *anybody,*" she pointed out with perfect truth.

"Does it matter?" Van's smile was extremely charming in its determined tolerance.

"Well, I rather think it does."

Terry laughed good-temperedly and explained to Mrs. Stacey:

"What Onslie means is that it just wouldn't have made any difference. Suppose Toby's mother had been—no better than she should be, for instance—and I suppose it's more than probable—still they would have wanted to have him."

It was not until that moment that Gwyneth realized how Toby had grown into Van's affections and pride. The look he gave Terry was quite frightening in its cold anger.

"I've never supposed Toby's mother to have been anything of the sort," he said icily, and for a moment an uncomfortable silence fell on the company.

Even when Mrs. Stacey healed the breach with a pleasant and cast-iron platitude, Gwyneth herself remained silent—withdrawn from the conversation, almost unbearably moved.

If Van had known! If Van had known! With those dear, curt, angry words, he had been defending his own wife. It touched her so that she could have wept in front of them all, and it hurt her that she would never be able to thank him for the comfort he had given her.

CHAPTER TEN

AFTER dinner, while Van and Terry were left with their host to do justice to his admirable port, Gwyneth found, to her dismay, that she was to inspect the part of Paula's trousseau which was already completed.

She didn't know which was more agitating—Paula's excited pleasure or her mother's graver, more weighty satisfaction.

The weaker part of her conscience began to whisper insistently to her: "Now, isn't it better to leave them in this nice fools' paradise as long as possible? They won't thank you for pushing them out of it. Is it really worth ruining your whole life to do it? Anyway, what *are* you going to do?"

She didn't know the answer to that question, so she looked at delectable creations in white and peach and palest blue and mauve, and said: "Sweet!" "How lovely!" and "What an adorable shade," as often as was necessary.

If only she had not known just how base Terry was! If only she hadn't seen for herself that his wife was still alive!

But of course, she ought not to think that, because it was that which had made her realize the urgent necessity of saving Paula.

It was ridiculous to suppose that Terry would really settle down with her for the rest of his life—even if one could overlook the unpleasant fact that the marriage was no marriage. That, after all, was not her business. But it *was* her business that she, of all of them, knew just what would happen when, presently, he grew tired of Paula. There would be nothing to hold him, either legally or financially. Her own parents would have provided him with the wherewithal to desert her.

And she would not be a deserted wife. She would be a deserted mistress—as Gwyneth had been. And there might be a child as well——

"Of course, I shall miss her very much." Mrs. Stacey was speaking and Gwyneth must listen and make suitable replies. "But it's what all parents must expect, sooner or later, and if you know your children are going to be happy, that really is the only thing that matters."

Gwyneth agreed as fervently as she could to this indisputably excellent truth. She wondered what good it would be to say: "Yes, but this man happens to be a bigamist, you know, and an extremely accomplished swindler."

No, that was not the way to do it. She must wait for a better opening.

Or was it just that her cowardly conscience counselled delay, delay, delay?

Back in the drawing-room once more, they found that the men had already come in, and presently Gwyneth sought the company of old Mr. Stacey, because she simply could not bear to hear the wedding and honeymoon plans which formed the principal part of almost every conversation conducted by Mrs. Stacey—or, indeed, Paula.

The old gentleman seemed pleased and rather flattered by her notice, and asked her if she played chess.

Gwyneth confessed complete ignorance, but was more than willing to show interest, if only it would keep him from the subject of Paula's foolish marriage.

He showed her his collection of chessmen, which included some beautiful specimens that she would have found genuinely interesting at any other time. They were at the far end of the long room now, rather removed from the others, and Gwyneth felt a slight slackening of the tension. It tightened almost immediately, however, when he said:

"Terry doesn't play, but he has a very keen appreciation of some of these specimens as works of art. I'm glad—I'm very glad, because I'd like them to go to someone who would appreciate them."

"Perhaps Paula would," Gwyneth suggested. (It was horrible! Even this nice old man's precious chessmen were to go to the contemptible, sponging Terry.)

He laughed slightly and shook his head.

"Oh no, Paula doesn't care much about this kind of thing. Naturally, naturally. She's very young and likes something brighter and more in keeping with youth. Besides"—his eyes twinkled—"it isn't a very feminine game, chess, you know."

"N-no. But if Terry is interested in these works of art, surely Paula might be too?"

"Oh, a little, I daresay. But she's more interested in jewellery and that sort of thing, you know. This is more what would have gone to a son, if we'd had one. But then, of course, Terry is a very good substitute for one. He's a good boy," the old man added, with grave inaccuracy. "We're more than willing to look on him *as* a son."

Gwyneth was silent, holding a beautifully-carved ivory 'piece' in her hand and trying to think what to say.

The old man watched her, willing to let her take her time in examining things.

"I suppose"—Gwyneth cleared her throat slightly, and started again—"I suppose you are perfectly satisfied about —Paula's future?"

"Pleased about her marriage, you mean?"

"Y-yes."

The old man smiled again, in the indulgent way he seemed to keep for any reference to his daughter.

"I think she is doing what will really make her happy, so—yes, I'm quite satisfied. I don't want to lose her, of course, but——"

"I didn't quite mean that."

"No? Well, I suppose you know he isn't bringing her very much in the way of worldly goods. In fact, it's very much the other way about, of course. I won't say the idea didn't shake me a good deal at first. That and his being an artist. I'd rather expected her to marry some decent, solid, comfortable fellow in the City. I suppose one always expects one's son-in-law to be in the same line as oneself. I shouldn't be surprised now, if your father had rather imagined you as a clergyman's wife?"

"Oh, I don't think so," Gwyneth said, a good deal surprised. She was perfectly sure her father hadn't had any ideas on the subject at all.

"Well, well, perhaps not. Anyway, it's rather a silly thing to do. It only means you have to readjust yourself when your girl does make her choice. And, of course, I did see Paula's point pretty quickly. One doesn't expect quite the same standards and ideas from an artist——"

"But one *does*," Gwyneth exclaimed in dismay. And then, before her slightly startled host could take that up, Van came over to her.

"I'm so sorry, Gwyn. I've just had a phone message and I shall have to go along to the office after all. But there is no need at all for you to come, of course. I'll take the car now, and I don't expect to be very long. As a matter of fact, I'm almost sure to get through in time to come back for you. If not, I daresay you won't mind getting a taxi."

"No, of course I don't mind." She spoke rather slowly, because she did mind, terribly. She felt frightened and deserted and alone. She knew some crisis was very close on her now. Ridiculous to feel like that, of course, because, if anything, it was better for Van *not* to be there. He could not be any help or protection—and in any case, he would be the worst person of all to have to tell. He would have to know about it—naturally—almost as soon as the others did—how, she was not quite sure; probably, she supposed, through Terry. But, in a way, it was something of a reprieve to have him go. She ought to feel glad.

But she didn't feel glad. She couldn't feel glad about anything. In a horrid sort of dream she saw him making the round of good-byes. He kissed her lightly—he never omitted to do that, however short the separation was to be. Then he went out of the room, and after a few minutes they heard the front door close.

For a little while after Van's departure, Gwyneth took in hardly anything of the conversation. She contributed a "Yes" and a "No" and a "Do you really think so?". But she was not paying very much attention to what was being said.

After a while she became aware that Terry was watching her with slightly narrowed eyes. She knew why, of course. He was judging her indecision to a nicety, and he knew his whole future depended on whether or not that indecision would harden into determination.

"Such a pity that Van had to go," Mrs. Stacey was saying. "The very first time we have been able to arrange a dinner party together. But I hope it will be only the first of many. When Paula is married, I dare say she will be entertaining us all in *her* house."

Benign and satisfied smiles came to bear upon Paula.

Slowly but irresistibly, Gwyneth saw, the moment was approaching. It was like hearing the rumblings of a volcano that was about to erupt.

"I can only say I hope Paula and Terry will be as happy as you and Van obviously are." Mrs. Stacey smiled benignly upon Gwyneth this time.

But Gwyneth didn't smile back. She looked straight across at Mrs. Stacey, her eyes so dark with fear and determination that they looked almost black, her face so white that her hostess gave an exclamation and half rose to her feet.

"It's all right, Mrs. Stacey. I expect I look ghastly, but I'm not going to faint or anything. Only there's something painful and horrible that I've got to say to you all——"

"Gwyneth!" The sharp word of protest came from Paula, not Terry. But Gwyneth took no notice.

"I've been trying to get up my courage to say this for nearly a week. It was wrong of me to wait so long—I did it because I was afraid. But nothing else is going to disclose the fact—I've got to do it. Terry can't legally marry Paula because he is married already, and his wife is alive. I know it because he played the same trick on me when I was even younger than she is. I can't stand by and see Paula put through the same experience—abandoned when he is tired of her, perhaps with a child—as I was."

"Gwyneth!" That was Paula again. "Are you mad? What

167

are you saying? You—with a child—— *Oh!* Do you mean that Toby——"

Gwyneth felt dreadfully cold, as she always did in a moment of despair and acute terror.

"Yes," she said slowly, "Toby is my own son—mine and Terry's."

There was such a profound silence for a few seconds after she had said that that she almost wondered if she had *really* said it, or if she were only following out the scene in her fevered imagination again—as she had so often done before.

Now that the confession was over, it scarcely seemed to hurt. It was like losing a limb and not being able to feel the loss at first because the nerves were numb.

Then Terry spoke—very coolly, but with a queer, metallic note in his voice.

"It's very distressing, of course, if Mrs. Onslie indulged in some such escapade years ago, but I most violently protest against having the result wished on to me."

"Terry, don't," Gwyneth said almost wearily. "It's so futile."

"Mrs. Onslie, these are terrible charges you're making against someone who is almost a member of our family." Mr. Stacey spoke in a voice which was really not quite steady. "I don't want to question your truthfulness, but—but you really must give us some form of proof, you know."

"I defy her to!" Terry was perfect in his rising tide of indignant annoyance. "It's an outrageous suggestion."

"No," Gwyneth said quietly, "it's not outrageous. The only outrageous part is your effrontery, Terry, when you must know you're beaten. Anyway, I *have* got proof."

Terry's eyes met hers for an instant in fear as well as anger. It was a strange moment—one that gave her a fierce, swift sense of triumph. It was gone almost as soon as it came, but it *had* been there. For the space of a couple of seconds she knew that Terry had been afraid of *her*, instead of the inevitable, humiliating reverse position.

She looked at him with measureless contempt.

"It was silly of you to leave me to pay the bill, all those years ago, for the weeks we spent together at that wretched

168

little hotel. Economical, perhaps, to leave it to me, but short-sighted. You see, I have the bill here."

She drew it out of her evening bag and spread it out on the small table beside her.

Very crumpled, slightly tattered from being crushed up at the bottom of a box for so long—it lay there for them all to see. Even now, she could not have said why she had kept it. Perhaps she had had some wild idea at the time that she might need it to prove something. Perhaps, having been cheated so often, she had merely thought that, at least, the shady hotel should not charge her again. Perhaps it was simply that some queer instinct had told her that, one day, it would be very important to her.

But anyway, there it was—damning evidence against even so accomplished a twister as Terry.

Three out of the four people present leant forward fascinatedly, to read the bill headed "Mr. and Mrs. T. Muirkirk".

"You can see—it's for quite a long period." Gwyneth still spoke with that sort of weary determination. "He'd had quite a good time before his wife came and claimed him. And if you want any further evidence, I suppose there is still some sort of record at the register office—false facts and all."

Again there was a heavy silence. Mr. Stacey, breathing rather deeply, slowly pulled the bill towards him and examined it afresh, as though something else might come to light.

Paula looked across at Terry with incredulous, horrified eyes.

"Is it true?" was all she said.

Even Terry must have seen this was the end. He shrugged.

"If you care to believe her word against mine——"

"But it isn't only her word. Here is the hotel bill, and—"

"Very well. It's perfectly true that we stayed there together for some weeks. I'm ashamed of it now, but you must know these things happen occasionally in a man's past, and he can only say that he wishes to God he'd never done it. The rest of her story is an invention, because she's never forgiven me for tiring of the whole wretched business long before she did."

"I think they feel more inclined to believe my version than yours, Terry," Gwyneth said quietly. "And Toby is no invention. Nor is your wife, who was walking with you when I saw you the other day. I suppose even you will find some difficulty in explaining her away."

Paula sprang to her feet. She was very white, but her eyes were brilliant with anger now, even more than with dismay. Gwyneth was astounded to see that, far from being crushed by the discovery, she seemed to take on a furious dignity before which Terry might well have trembled.

"How dare you!" she said slowly. "How dare you come here, lying and cheating and—yes, sponging. I could—I could kill you!" And suddenly all the composure went. She burst into wild tears, more like a furious child again, and rushed from the room.

Her mother gave an agitated little exclamation, and, getting up, she went after her. At the door, she turned and addressed her husband, a little as though Terry and—to tell the truth, Gwyneth—no longer existed.

"I hope, William, you will deal with this—this *person*," she said, and went out of the room, too.

"I think," Mr. Stacey said—and, small man though he was, he looked almost dignified in his turn as he addressed Terry—"I think you will see that to remain here in our house would be both pointless and offensive."

Terry bowed slightly, even now concealing what must have been very deep chagrin under an insolent little smile.

"Since you put it so pressingly as that, I'll go."

He bowed slightly to Gwyneth, too, but the cold menace in his eyes made her very heart quail. He looked like a murderer at that moment. Only a tremendous physical effort kept her from letting him see how afraid she was, but she managed to stare back coolly at him until he turned away.

Even when he had gone out of the room, Mr. Stacey didn't say anything to her at once. He sat down rather heavily, his elbows resting on his knees, his hands hanging aimlessly. He looked a very old man indeed just then.

They both heard the clang of the front door closing behind Terry. He had gone out of Paula's life now. But out of Gwyneth's life, too——? Well, that was a different thing.

Gwyneth looked at the bent old man, and hated the fact that it had been she who had had to deal this blow.

"Mr. Stacey, I feel I ought to say how terribly sorry I am that——"

He roused himself then to interrupt her before she could finish her lame little apology.

"My dear, it was not your fault that such dreadful facts were there to be told. It was extremely brave of you to tell them. I—we appreciate what it must have meant for you to rake up such an unhappy story—something that was entirely your own affair. It was very, very good of you to put Paula's welfare before your own feelings like that. I know my wife would feel the same. She would want me to say this for her, as well as for myself."

Gwyneth smiled rather wanly at him.

"Thank you—but I couldn't have done anything else really, you know. No one could, without being absolutely despicable."

The old man shook his head.

"It was a very severe demand of conscience, and I should like you to feel sure——" He paused and looked slightly embarrassed. "That is to say, I hope you understand that in no circumstances should we ever abuse the confidence you've placed in us. What you told us belongs to your own past history, and yours alone. Please consider that it is absolutely safe with us."

"Thank you," Gwyneth said again, and she took the hand which he held out to her.

She didn't tell him that it was not they whom she feared, but Terry. She held his hand very warmly for a moment. Then she managed to smile more naturally.

"I think I had better go, Mr. Stacey. I don't expect that either Paula or Mrs. Stacey will want to see anyone again tonight."

"Oh, but please let me fetch my wife. She would want——"

"No, really." Gwyneth was firm. "Paula will need her. I don't want her to feel she must come down again."

"But do wait until Van comes to fetch you. He said he

171

would come for you. I don't like the idea of your going alone."

"It's really quite all right," Gwyneth assured him, contriving somehow to disguise from him her wild longing to escape—escape, away from this terrible house, where this awful thing had happened to her.

"If you're quite sure——"

"Quite sure. I shall be home before Van starts out to fetch me."

"But he'll come straight from the office."

"Oh yes, of course he will." She was given pause for a moment—forced to think out some other way of keeping Van from returning here. She didn't want him back at this house, tonight. She didn't want further conferences and explanations just now. She was prepared to face the wretched fact that he must know. But now now—not for a few hours longer. She had had as much as she could bear.

She turned back to Mr. Stacey.

"If I might telephone, please——?"

"Of course, of course."

He dialed the number for her, and she was sorry to see that his rather withered hands were very unsteady. Then she took the receiver, and the next moment she heard Van himself say:

"Yes? Van Onslie speaking."

"Van, it's Gwyneth. Look here, dear, don't bother to come for me. I'm getting a taxi now." Her voice was amazingly calm and matter-of-fact, she noticed.

"Now?" She could almost see him glance in surprise at his watch. "But it's very early yet, isn't it?"

"Yes, I know. I'll explain later. Just go straight home, Van. I'll join you there."

"Very well, of course, if you really want that."

"Yes, please." She rang off quickly, then, for fear he might ask questions, though she thought from his tone that he had gathered there was something which she could not explain by telephone.

When she had rung off, she found old Mr. Stacey watching her with a grave and troubled expression. But he said comfortingly:

"Van will make you feel less unhappy, my dear. All this did happen a good many years ago, and now that you are

172

happily married you must put everything behind you again. It was terrible that you had to look back like that, but since you were brave enough to do it, I hope you will be brave enough to forget it again now. I am sure Van would be the first to remind you that you have your little boy safely with you now, and Van is evidently extremely fond of him as well as of you. Nothing *could* have worked out better——"

"Except," Gwyneth said sadly, "that Van doesn't know anything about this at all. He has no idea that Toby is my own child—and Terry's."

The consternation on Mr. Stacey's face was an eloquent comment on what he thought Van's reaction would be. For a moment he obviously could think of nothing at all to say.

"I didn't realize that," he murmured at last, shaking his head. "I didn't understand that, at all. Oh, dear, dear, this is terrible." Then he added—not very hopefully: "We must hope that Terry will, at least, have the decency to keep things to himself."

Gwyneth sighed. "No," she said, "I'm afraid decency doesn't enter into Terry's calculations at all. He kept quiet until now because, of course, he couldn't expose my story without showing his own part in it. If he were really going to marry Paula, it was as much in his interests as in mine that he should say nothing. But now——"

She broke off without finishing the sentence, and she and Mr. Stacey looked at each other in silence. It was so difficult to think of anything to say.

"Of course, Van is a very *just* man," Mr. Stacey offered at last, but he evidently didn't think much of that feeble bit of comfort himself.

"It's a little difficult to be strictly just, when everything you admire and cherish is involved," Gwyneth said. "I think perhaps it is mercy rather than justice that is needed."

"Of course, of course." There was a short silence. Neither of them offered to say what the chances were of Van displaying mercy in a situation like this.

"He really has *no* idea at all?" the old man said at last. "No, none."

"It will be a terrible shock. You must try not to mind

173

too much, my dear, if he—if he says some very hard things at first."

Gwyneth didn't answer. She thought she could bear it if he only spoke to her. The terrible, burning question was —what would he *do?*

What did a man do when he found his wife had had a 'past'? But it wasn't any good putting it into general terms like that. A 'past' didn't necessarily involve a child—now living under the unsuspecting husband's roof.

This story did.

But it was no good lingering on here, going over possibilities and impossibilities. It was strange enough, now she came to think of it, that she should have spent so much time, talking over her most intimate affairs with this old gentleman whom she had never met until this evening. But he was sympathetic, and she had had to talk to *someone*. And, in any case, the privacy of her affairs seemed rather a small thing just now.

She said good-bye to Mr. Stacey after that, begging him to make her good-byes for her to Paula and her mother. He came with her to the taxi—very anxious, very kind, wishing he could do something for her.

But no one could do anything for her. That was the worst part of it. Her worried host could only clasp her hand very warmly as he said good night, and bow to her in a way that suggested she was really not at all to be despised, even if she had just described a most unhappy scandal in her past.

She was alone at last—leaning back in the taxi with her eyes closed, trying not to remember the more awful moments of the evening.

And now she had to think what she was going to do about Van.

Well, she didn't know, of course. Her mind seemed to move very slowly and laboriously, and not to light upon anything at all helpful. She supposed, really, that the most obvious course was to go in now and confess the whole thing to him.

And yet——

Suppose Terry, by some miracle, did *not* speak—did not betray her. Or suppose he failed to reach Van with what he had to say——

The taxi stopped with a jerk.

She got out mechanically, paid the driver and felt for her latch-key. As she opened the door of the flat, Van came out of the sitting-room to meet her.

"Hello, my dear. What happened?"

He gently took her fur coat from her and, putting his arm round her, went with her into the room.

"It was just that something very—unfortunate and—horrid happened," Gwyneth returned his kiss almost absently, and sank down in a chair by the fire. (He wouldn't have kissed her if he had known! Perhaps that was the last time he ever *would* kiss her.)

"Something which really upset you, do you mean?" He was standing looking down at her, tenderly and a little anxiously.

"Well—it was such a distressing business for all of them. They—Paula found out, just in the nick of time, that Terry is really married already——"

"Married!"

"—And that he makes almost a practice of this sort of thing—going round and apparently marrying rich, credulous young women. When he had had enough of Paula he —he meant to clear off, taking with him the money that Mr. Stacey would have settled on him. It was all quite— quite simple. They had helped to remove any obstacle themselves by being so very trusting."

"Good God! Then you were right in your instinct."

"What instinct?" She pushed back her hair wearily.

"When you said you felt certain Muirkirk was a bad type and meant Paula no good. What an extraordinary thing! You were absolutely right."

She swallowed slightly. How was she to tell him that instinct had played no part—only sordid experience?

"But how on earth did the whole thing come out?— And what is going to happen now?"

"Well, of course, he had to go, and there is no question of his ever coming back," Gwyneth said slowly, taking the second question first. "He was—recognized by someone, Van."

"Recognized? By someone who just happened to call, do you mean? What an amazing coincidence! But how confoundedly lucky, too. Why, Paula's whole life would

175

have been ruined. I suppose she's taken it pretty badly, poor kid?"

"I'm afraid—she has," Gwyneth agreed faintly.

"Well, of course, it's a horrible experience for any girl to have—though nothing like so horrible as if she had gone on and married him. This she can get over. She's young. She'll recover by and by, and find some other really nice fellow. She's much too attractive not to, and Paula's type is very elastic, with plenty of recuperative power."

"Yes."

She was dully thankful that, for some reason or other, he chose this particular moment to talk rather more than was usual with him. It gave her a slight chance of recovering herself.

Everything was not yet over. By a hair's breadth she had slipped past disaster once more. He was satisfied with the explanation she had given—which *he* had practically given, come to that. He had almost put the words into her mouth. The relief——

But she knew suddenly that this time it was not relief. It was, rather, a dull horror that the thing was *not* over. Unless she could tell him in cold blood herself—and how could she? How could she? She must go on dragging about this dead weight of fear and anticipation for some days longer, waiting until the blow fell.

Useless to tell herself she might just as well confess now and get it over, because in a day—two days, Terry would do it for her. With a frantic effort at self-preservation, she still clung to the hundredth, thousandth, millionth chance that something would save her.

Look how it had done so far! Why, if she had spoken when she first wanted to——

"Look here, darling, I'll tell you what I'm going to do with you," Van's concerned voice recalled her to the present. "I'm going to send you off to bed here and now. You're looking absolutely done. You mustn't upset yourself so much, you know, over other people's problems." He bent down and lifted her right up out of the chair.

She locked her arms convulsively round his neck and kissed him and kissed him.

"It's horrible when it happens, I know," he said gently.

"But Paula will get over it, and so will her parents. After the first shock, one couldn't be anything but thankful for the escape."

"I know—I know." It was only a whisper, and spoken almost against him.

He carried her to her room then, waited to see that she would really undress and go straight to bed, and then went to get her a hot drink himself.

When he came back again, she was lying in bed—very quiet and a little pale still, but she contrived to give him a brilliant smile as he came in.

She heard him catch his breath in a slight sound of relief, and that made her want to cry and to cling round him again, telling him all that had really happened. It was not only that she wanted the relief of some sort of confession herself. In this moment she hated and despised herself for ever having lied to someone who trusted her, as Van did now.

She had never liked the idea of living a lie—or, rather, of having deliberately suppressed the truth. But somehow, the real baseness of it had never quite come home to her in those early days, when his cool, rather hard and autocratic manner had been a perpetual reminder of his strength.

Now, for a few unhappy minutes, she had the dreadful feeling of having exploited someone whose very love for her put him at a disadvantage. It was not a nice sensation.

"As well as everything else," thought Gwyneth, "it's been mean—mean—mean. How I hate myself—and I wish I were dead."

But Van didn't wish her dead. He wished her alive—very much so. He was anxious about her—wanted to do a dozen things for her comfort and to make her rest better.

"I'm all right, Van dear. I'm quite all right." She couldn't tell him, of course, that it only hurt all the more to have him so sweet and attentive.

He left her at last, in the belief that she was on the verge of falling asleep. And she was free to lie there, staring into the darkness, wondering how much more she could bear of this sickening uncertainty and subterfuge.

CHAPTER ELEVEN

THE next few days were so terrible that Gwyneth could never afterwards remember them individually. They just seemed one long nightmare stretch of dreariness and tension and cracking nerves.

Every time the telephone bell rang she felt a chill crawl down her spine, and each time the post arrived she would try—hating and despising herself the while—to see if there were a letter in Terry's handwriting, so that she could perhaps remove it before Van saw it.

On the afternoon of the third day Paula came to see her. She had not telephoned first, and Gwyneth rather thought that the visit was made on impulse.

She was quiet and subdued and not at all given to any of her usual flippancies. With a good deal of pity, Gwyneth saw that she was still suffering badly from the shock of Terry's exposure. She did not, however appear to have any illogical animus against Gwyneth for having so painfully opened her eyes.

Her greeting to Gwyneth had all its usual affection—rather more, perhaps, since it was altogether quieter and more sincere.

"I've been wanting so much to see you, Gwyn dear," she said, and she obviously meant it. "I felt I had to come in and talk to you."

"I'm glad," Gwyneth clasped her hand very tightly. "I was afraid you would feel you could never dissociate me from—from what happened, and that you might never want to see me again." And she smiled rather ruefully.

"What! blame *you* because *I* had made an utter fool of myself? Even I am not so illogical as that."

Paula seemed rather bent on abasing herself, and Gwyneth hastily came to her rescue.

"No, no, I didn't mean anything like that. You didn't make a fool of yourself, anyway. You couldn't possibly have guessed the real state of affairs."

"You tried to tell me, right in the beginning," Paula spoke a little bitterly. "I've been remembering that in the last few days. And I just wouldn't listen to you."

Gwyneth shrugged and smiled faintly again.

"I don't know that anyone else would have listened in

the circumstances, Paula. I suppose it was a little unreasonable to tell you only a quarter of the story, and then expect you to feel as I did. But I—I *couldn't*——"

"No I know. Gwyneth"—Paula looked embarrassed, a most unusual thing with her—"I want to say that I'm most frightfully sorry that, in the end, you were forced out into the open like that. These things are absolutely no one's business except one's own and—and I'm so sorry you had to tell us the whole story before I would understand."

"It doesn't matter," Gwyneth said, and she realized in that moment that it didn't. "Somehow, I can't mind any more about anything like wondering what people think of me. I can only think of the terrible, grim essentials, such as when Van will find out and what he will do when he does know."

"He may never know, Gwyn."

"Terry will tell him, if it's the last thing he ever does."

"See him, you mean?"

"N-no. I think he knows Van would kill him if he said such a thing to his face. He'll phone or write, I suppose. But when — when — when?" Gwyneth stopped herself abruptly, realizing that she was not very far from hysteria.

"But if he writes, Gwyn, can't you stop the letter?" Paula asked anxiously.

"Oh, I try to see the post first, of course. But how I hate these mean sordid tricks! To think that the happiness of my marriage depends on my tampering with my husband's letters! It's so degrading. I know myself for a weak, small-minded woman, when I find myself reduced to that sort of thing. I ought to have had the courage to tell him long ago. I can see it now. A big character would have. I've just let myself be pushed from one shameful emergency to another, and now I'm so ashamed of the whole story that I don't know which is the worst part of it."

Paula stared at her in silent dismay.

"You're not weak and small-minded," she said at last, having seized on that phrase of Gwyneth's bitter outburst. "No one who was weak and small-minded would have done what you did the other night."

"Oh yes, they would, Paula dear. They would have done it long before I did, too. I caused a great deal of unnecessary suffering for you because I was too much of a coward

179

to say anything until the very, very last minute. I kept on hoping that some impossible miracle would put things right without my having to do anything."

"Well, hang it, Gwyn! I don't wonder. It was a pretty tough thing to have to do. I'm not at all sure that I could have done it if things had been the other way round. *Anyone* would have gone on hoping against hope that something would happen."

"But it's so futile to do that."

"It's very human," Paula said feelingly.

"You're a good child, Paula—not to blame me in the least."

"Blame you! Why on earth should I blame you? I think it was darned sporting of you to save me from my own idiocy, at such a price."

"I meant—about my delaying so long. It—it does hurt so awfully. I know, when you've made so many plans and—quite suddenly—the whole thing comes to pieces in your hand."

"Y-yes. But that's better than a long-drawn-out disillusionment, I suppose," Paula said with unusual wisdom. "Besides——" She broke off, looking slightly embarrassed again. Then she went on more slowly. "I don't know whether I'm an awfully shallow person, or whether it's just that the shock was so terrific that it removed everything, but—I can't feel heartbroken. That's all there is about it. I know girls don't often own to these things, but what's the good of pretending? Terry, as I thought of him, just didn't exist. He's simply a cadging swindler, whom I didn't know. I'm sore about it all, of course, and there's a lot of disappointment about it somewhere, but——" Again she left the sentence unfinished, but this time an expressive shrug filled the gap.

Gwyneth looked at her with kindly eyes. She had never liked Paula more than at this moment. There was something so downright about her, so determined not to sentimentalize over her feelings or pretend to an interesting broken heart. Facts were facts to Paula. It was stupid to make them into something different for the sake of effect.

"I don't think you're shallow, Paula dear," Gwyneth said. "It's what Van said—you have an elastic temperament, and you make good recoveries. I know it's sickening when people smile superiorly and say there'll be someone else later on, but—I expect there will be. You're a very pretty girl and much too common sense and lovable not to make lots more friends."

Paula made a little face.

"Nice of you to say so, and it does something to restore my bruised *amour propre*. But I expect I shall have to do any more romancing among Daddy's chess-playing contemporaries. They're about the only males I see in the ordinary way—and poor Mother will be more careful than ever now."

"Oh, nonsense. We'll see to it that you do quite a lot ——" Gwyneth stopped, a queer contraction of her throat holding back the rest of her sentence. What chance would she have to 'see to it' that Paula 'did quite a lot of things'? —how could she speak of 'we'? Next week, tomorrow, tonight even, Van might perhaps know everything. And that would be the end.

Gwyneth didn't know quite what she thought 'the end' would mean. She wavered between some idea of being turned out of the flat with Toby, and having to stay on and on instead, doing all the things she had always done, but with every dear, familiar detail meaning nothing any longer. All dead sea fruit because Van would no longer love her.

Paula didn't say anything. It was obvious that she understood the sudden silence which had fallen, and it was equally obvious that she could think of no comfort to offer. Only when Gwyneth shivered convulsively did she manage to say rather feebly:

"Maybe it won't ever happen, after all, Gwyn." But she didn't sound very well convinced of that herself.

Soon after tea Paula left, and as Van had not come in from the office yet, Gwyneth had a quiet half-hour with Toby. She had not realized how closely the child watched her, until he came now and put his hand on her knee, and said:

"Mummy, do you feel sick?"

The deep, anxious little voice touched her, even while she smiled:

"No, darling."

"Have you got a headache?"

"Oh no. I'm quite all right, thank you," she assured him. He wagged his head solemnly.

"*I* don't think you're all right. I think you're ill. You don't talk much and you don't laugh *at all*."

She smiled then.

"Am I so dull? I'm sorry, Toby."

"Not dull, Mummy. Sad. Shall I come and sit beside you?"

"Please." She made room for him in the big chair, and he got up beside her.

"Isn't this nice?" he said, and she agreed that it was.

Dear little cause of half the trouble! And yet she would not have been without him for the world.

"I think you're sad because Daddy's late," Toby said at last, having worked things out to his own satisfaction.

"Perhaps that's it." Gwyneth dropped a kiss on the top of his bright head.

"He says the same about you. He's sad when you're not there."

"Is he? Did he say that?" She was smiling now. It was amusing and touching to think of Van and Toby discussing her.

"Yes. He says you're like the little man in the weather house. When you are there it's fine weather, and when you go away again it rains."

"Oh, Toby, did he really say that?" She hugged the little boy against her. "I do love you both so much," she exclaimed. "I don't know what I should do if I lost either of you."

"You couldn't lose us," Toby said. "We'd come back. If I got lost I should go to a policeman. Betty said I must, and I like policemen."

"Yes, yes, of course."

"I expect Daddy would go to a policeman, too. But he always knows the way home, doesn't he?"

Gwyneth couldn't quite answer that because there was a lump in her throat. She kissed Toby instead. And after that they were silent for a while. Toby was a restful child, and he lay there quite contentedly in the circle of her arm, gradually growing more and more sleepy.

She put Toby to bed herself that night, and when——half-way through the solemn rite—Van telephoned to say he would be very late, Toby said:

"I'd better stay and keep you company."

That really did make Gwyneth laugh.

"No, no, pet. You go to bed and to sleep. I shall be quite all right," she assured him. But he came and ate his supper with her in the lounge, and in the end he had 'ten minutes extra'.

When he was finally in bed, and she had had a solitary dinner, Gwyneth sat by the fire, trying to read, but finding, every few minutes, that her own thoughts came between her and the book.

What a dear, good child Toby was! Not in the least like his wretched father. Nor, come to that, like his mother.

"We haven't shown many good qualities between us, to pass on to him," Gwyneth thought rather bitterly. "I wish I could have been an example to him. Someone decent and courageous and dependable. It was good of Paula to say I wasn't weak and small-minded—but oh, I wish I could have been something worthwhile!"

It must be wonderful to be the sort of parent children were proud of as they grew up. The sort of parent who set a high standard and kept unflinchingly to it. That made things so much easier for children. They grow up then with the idea that one simply didn't do anything but the brave, decent thing.

Toby would never know, of course, what had really happened, but he would sense instinctively that Van despised her and had lost his trust in her. That was—if Van decided to stay with them at all.

"I wish he would come in," Gwyneth thought.

And then—"No, I don't. While he's not here, at least I don't have to go on pretending and pretending. I can be myself—let my fears and doubts show."

But it was silly to indulge those too far. They took hold of one more and more, destroyed the miserable bit of nerve one had left. Better not think about those things any more. She could do nothing, anyway. Nothing, nothing, nothing. It was out of her hands.

She read determinedly again, but a few minutes later, the sound of the postman roused her. She sat there rigid, staring at the page and seeing nothing, straining her ears while Betty came out of her room and went to the front door. In a minute she would bring the letters in here. One would remain perfectly calm, of course—show no sign that something more dangerous than a bomb might be among the letters——

"The post, madam." Betty came in and put the letters on the small table at Gwyneth's elbow.

She glanced up and smiled slightly.

"Oh, thank you, Betty." She spoke with admirable carelessness as she picked up the letters. "Not very many tonight, are there? I expect——" She never finished saying what she expected. She was staring down at the last letter of the pile.

She knew Terry's writing too well to make any mistake. And the letter was addressed to Van.

When Betty had gone, Gwyneth sat there, perfectly still for a long while, the unopened letter in her hand.

It was here at last—the horror which she had dreaded. This evening, of all evenings, it had come—and she had a perfect opportunity of destroying it—unread.

It was so simple that there must be a flaw in it somewhere. And yet she could see none.

She had only to put the letter in the fire, watch it burn —and then the whole business was over.

Or nearly so.

She glanced at the postmark on the letter. Southampton! Then it was, at least, likely that he was leaving the country —having made it a little too hot to hold him. This was his last shot, fired when he was already almost out of reach. He would hardly risk waiting for Van to find him out.

Gwyneth didn't know why she was hesitating like this. The chance of saving herself was even more complete than anything she had imagined.

She wished she didn't remember so painfully her bitter protest to Paula—"To think that the happiness of my marriage depends on my tampering with my husband's letters!"

Small, mean, dishonourable makeshifts—those were the things by which she lived. Stolen letters, specious lies, daily prevarication.

"What have I really come to?" Gwyneth spoke aloud.

Then she lay back almost exhaustedly in her chair, holding the letter more slackly now, her eyes closed.

The man who loved her and lived with her believed every word she said. He had told Paula that she was 'as perfect as it was possible for a woman to be without becoming uninteresting'. And to Toby he had said that when she was there the sun shone and when she went away it rained.

That was how he thought of her. That was how he believed in her. And she was sitting here now, deciding to burn a letter addressed to him because she was afraid of his knowing the truth about her.

After that, she would go on from day to day again, hoping that nothing would betray her—lying here, pretending there, watching his post still in case Terry wrote again and she had to do a little more letter-stealing.

Oh, it was so contemptible—so mean! And she had been thinking just now how wonderful it must be to be an example to one's children.

Van himself would never have stooped to any sort of lie, she knew. He would have been much to proud.

But then nothing frightened him—it was partly that, she supposed. But only partly. To Van it was just impossible to work things out on a mean scale.

Van was the kind of a parent she wished Toby could have had. In a way, Toby was more like Van's child than hers. A good, earnest little thing—unafraid and completely straightforward.

"How horrible! I'm just not worthy of them. Not worthy of either my husband or my child," Gwyneth thought.

She opened her eyes again and looked once more at the letter.

The choice was hers. Quite clearly and ruthlessly she saw that now. She could burn the letter and go on living her lie with a fair measure of contemptible safety. Or she could tell the truth from the beginning.

It would lay her life in ruins, of course. "But oh, they would be clean ruins," thought Gwyneth with a sob. And, at that moment, there was the sound of Van's key in the door.

She was standing when he came into the room, pale and quiet, but with the air of strained desperation gone.

"I'm sorry I'm so late, Gwyn." He came over and kissed her. "Have you been very lonely?"

"Oh no. It's all right. I had Toby and then—then I was reading."

He dropped into the chair she had just vacated, and she sat down then on the rug at his feet.

"The babe all right?" He reached for his letters, a little wearily, she thought, and he frowned impatiently as he flicked them over.

"Oh yes, Toby's quite all right. I let him stay up an extra ten minutes because he said I needed someone to keep me company."

Van laughed and pushed his letters away again.

"Nothing important there," he said carelessly and, leaning back in his chair, he looked at her with very great pleasure, as though the sight of her rested him.

Gwyneth somehow stilled her nervous trembling. She must be calm, she told herself—not at all hysterical.

Slowly she took out the letter from the front of her dress where she had thrust it.

"Van, there was another letter for you. Here it is."

He took it from her with a puzzled frown and looked at it.

"It's from Terry," she said baldly.

He didn't open it at once.

"Why had you got it there?" he asked.

"I didn't—really—want you—to read it."

"Didn't you?" Van looked at her again. "Well then, I don't think," he said slowly, "that I will."

And, leaning forward, he put the letter in the fire.

With fascinated eyes she watched the flames curl round the letter. It was burning—as she had wanted it to burn.

She thought her heart would burst—with relief, with her love for Van, and then with the certain knowledge that she could not accept rescue this way.

With a terrible little sob, she leant her head against his knee and began to cry despairingly.

"It won't do," she sobbed forlornly. "It won't do that way, at all."

"What won't do, my darling?"

He was bending forward now, stroking her hair very lightly but not attempting to stop her tears.

186

"There's something—I've got—to tell you."

He didn't say anything. He just waited.

"It's about—Toby."

She felt him stiffen.

"Oh, Van, Van—I thought I knew every way of telling you and now I can't remember anything but the crude fact. He's mine—my own child. Toby is my son."

There was a long silence. Then Van said quietly:

"Don't cry, my dearest. I know. I've known almost from the beginning."

CHAPTER TWELVE

GWYNETH was absolutely still.

The silence was so profound that it seemed to be in her very soul. It was like standing on the edge of the world and looking into eternity.

Then she felt Van gather her up in his arms, and she was lifted on to his knee and held very close against him.

Even then nothing was said between them for a long while. At last she said in a very small whisper:

"How did you know?"

He didn't answer at once. When he did, he spoke very thoughtfully, as though he were recalling each step carefully.

"I think I had some sort of instinctive suspicion even before the idea became coherent," he said slowly. "I knew Toby had some significance for you, or that he would *become* something very important. I didn't very much like the idea. That was why I was very curt with you that first day when you spoke of wanting to have him home. I was a beast to you, wasn't I?" He put his cheek against the top of her head.

"Oh no, you were never a beast to me—never anything but kind and dear and wonderful."

He laughed softly.

"The description doesn't seem to fit exactly, but never mind."

"Tell me how you found out for certain."

"It was at the time of the fire. When you fainted and were unconscious all that long time, I think the last idea

187

in your mind must have been that you had called to Toby to jump——"

"Yes, it was. I did call him, you know. I told him I would catch him."

"Yes. But when you went over and over it again, you didn't use the same words, darling. You kept on saying: 'Jump, Toby, jump! Mother will catch you.' "

"Oh, Van——" The slow tears came into her eyes. "Did I really say that?"

"I don't know how, but I *knew*, from the first moment, that you were not expressing some fancy or even a wish. It was the literal truth. You were his mother. I tried to tell myself that people in delirium say the queerest things. It wasn't any good. I knew Toby was your child—and that that was why he tugged at my heart every time I looked at him."

She turned and kissed him, wonderingly and rather timidly.

"I don't know how—you can say—these things."

"Because they are true, Gwyn. What's the good of my pretending? I couldn't love you as I do and not love your child, too."

She pressed against him in silent gratitude. It was how she herself had argued—hopefully, hopelessly. Pretending it might happen, because she wanted it so terribly—yet knowing in her heart that nothing so wonderful ever could really happen.

"Van"—she couldn't look at him even now—"didn't you feel absolutely terrible at first?"

"Yes," he said slowly. "I think, in any other circumstances, I should have told myself that I wanted to kill you. But I couldn't indulge in such dramatics then, Gwyn, because, you see, you were really very near death—so near that I had a foretaste of what it would be like if I did lose you. You were much more ill than we ever told you. I sat beside you all that evening, while, very forlornly, you condemned yourself over and over again, out of your own mouth. At first I only thought how terrible it was. Then I began to see how pitiful it was, too. I *had* to listen. I had no choice. And gradually I began to understand a little of your secret longing for your baby and your certainty that you could never have him."

He was silent for a minute, as though he were recalling his own feelings at the time. Then he went on:

"I don't know how or why, Gwyn—because I'm not at all a forgiving man—but there came over me then the absolute longing to give you what you wanted so piteously. I wanted you to have your little boy, so that you could never grieve in that terrible way again."

She was crying once more, but much more softly and quietly this time.

He stroked her hair again.

"Don't cry, love. I had a lot to learn, too, you know."

"Oh no!" she whispered. "No. You've always been as you are now. Understanding and just and—almost great, Van."

"No, dear. I thought at first, 'I'll let her have the child, of course, but nothing will ever be the same again.' "

"It was natural to think that."

He shook his head slightly.

"It didn't last. It was like my melodramatic assertion once that I should want to wring the neck of any man I knew had kissed you."

"Oh, Van, I often thought of that. It used to make me so frightened and ashamed. I used to wonder whatever you would do to me if you found out. You don't know how I pretended and deceived and stooped to all sorts of little half truths because I was too much of a coward to tell you the truth."

"I'm sorry, darling. I forced you into all that."

"No, no, Van! That's absurd. It was only because I was so weak."

He kissed the side of her wet cheek, but she was not crying any more now.

"I know how you felt," he said, "because I remember how *I* felt in the beginning, and you probably thought of that as being the only way I could react. But, Gwyn, that all changed very soon. I found that it wasn't only that I wanted you to have Toby—I didn't want you humiliated and frightened by having to confess anything. I wanted everything put behind us, and to let you be happy in the way you *could* be happy."

"My dear! Was that why you wouldn't let Dr. Kellaby look up the few facts they had about Toby?"

"Yes. You were terribly frightened when he suggested it, weren't you?"

She nodded.

"Oh, Van! No wonder it seemed that so often some strange coincidence saved me."

"Um-hm." He smiled as though it gave him great pleasure to remember that. "I was the coincidence."

She even laughed a little then and pressed close against him.

"Did you *really* feel no bitterness after a while?"

"I thought, Gwyn, that it would be quite all right, so long as I never had to know who the man was."

She stiffened sharply and he must have felt it, because his arms pressed her reassuringly.

"All right, darling. Even that didn't work out as I expected. I was rather a fool about Terry. I ought to have guessed long before, but I didn't. Perhaps some vague suspicion was there, but the certainty came quite suddenly—"

"When?"

"That evening at Paula's place when the skunk said that about—Toby's mother."

"Oh, Van—oh, Van! You're so dear. Was *that* why you were so angry? I thought how terribly, terribly touching it was that you should be defending me without even knowing that it was I. But it's much more touching that you should have done it intentionally."

"I wanted to get up and hit him then and there, but that wouldn't have been any real service to you, of course. And by the time I'd controlled the impulse, I found that it didn't matter a damn whether I knew the man or not. You were *my* darling and you always would be. You were mine to love and protect. I didn't want you to abase yourself or explain or feel wretched. I only wanted you to be happy and feel that you were safe with me and the baby."

"If I'd know! If I'd known!" And then she smiled slowly. "No—I'm glad I didn't know. I'm glad I told you, however late it was and however cowardly I have been. To be rescued is one thing, but to work out your own—your own salvation is another. I'm glad I had to tell you—and to tell you at the only moment when it had become unnecessary. There's something like poetic justice in it."

He smiled at that and drew her down against him once more.

She lay there for a long while, gazing into the fire, and slowly, slowly allowing the cool, sweet truth to penetrate every corner of her fevered mind. He knew—Van knew everything—and yet it was all right. She would never have to be afraid again. Never scheme and pretend, while, all the time, the weight of guilt pressed upon her like a physical burden.

Almost as though it were unimportant she said presently:

"I did think he'd married me, you know. I didn't really mean to do anything wicked."

"Oh, darling." He kissed her. "Don't. You break my heart. You're not in the least wicked."

It was so good—it was so good to have Van's word for that.

"I'm so happy," she whispered. "Thank you, Van. It's you who have given me my happiness."

"I could not ask any sweeter reward," he said slowly.

"Don't you really ask anything but that? Just to know my happiness is secure?"

He smiled.

"Yours and Toby's."

"And what about your own?"

"That *is* my happiness," he told her, and, bending his head, he kissed her very tenderly.

EACH MONTH –
FOUR GREAT NOVELS

Here are the Latest Titles:

These titles are available at your local bookseller, or through the Harlequin Reader Service, M.P.O. Box 707, Niagara Falls, N.Y. 14302; Canadian address 649 Ontario St., Stratford, Ont. N5A 6W4.